THE DUKE & THE VICAR'S DAUGHTER

The Duke of Edbury decides he must marry an heiress if he is to save his estates. So far he has managed to stay out of the clutches of the predatory mothers who spend the Season searching for suitable husbands for their daughters. The goddaughter of his aunt, Lady Patience, might be a suitable candidate, and he is persuaded to act as a temporary guardian to both her and her cousin, Charity Lawson. When Charity and Patience exchange places, the fun begins . . .

FENELLA J. MILLER

THE DUKE & THE VICAR'S DAUGHTER

Complete and Unabridged

LINFORD
Leicester

First published in Great Britain in 2014

First Linford Edition
published 2015

A catalogue record for this book is available
from the British Library.

ISBN 978–1–4448–2587–9

Published by
F. A. Thorpe (Publishing)
Anstey, Leicestershire

Set by Words & Graphics Ltd.
Anstey, Leicestershire
Printed and bound in Great Britain by
T. J. International Ltd., Padstow, Cornwall

This book is printed on acid-free paper

1

Charity tossed her book to one side in disgust. She really must stop borrowing this nonsense from her cousin, Patience, who was addicted to silly romances. Mama had taken the little ones to visit a neighbour and Papa was busy writing his sermon for next Sunday's service.

As the weather was clement for February she decided to put on her stout walking boots and trudge across the fields to visit Bromley Hall. Although her mother's twin sister had become a countess when she married the Earl of Bromley, she stood on no ceremony and was always delighted to see her poor relations.

With the hood of her warm cloak pulled up, mittens on and a thick woollen muffler wrapped around her neck she was certain she would be unbothered by the elements. She knocked on the study door. 'Papa, I'm going to see

Patience, I'll be back before it gets dark.'

Her father looked up and smiled. 'Be careful, my dear, don't fall in any ditches this time.'

'Please don't remind me, Papa, I've never been so embarrassed in my life. Do you wish me to fetch you a hot drink before I leave?'

'No, thank you. Polly will take good care of me in your absence.' He gestured towards the door. 'I take it the rest of our family have gone out — it's blessedly quiet out there.'

'They have. With luck, you won't be disturbed until teatime. Don't work too hard, Papa.'

There was no maid to accompany her; they only had a cook-housekeeper and two girls to run the ancient rectory. Mama and she took care of their own clothes but fortunately they had Mary as nursemaid for her siblings. Charity had never liked to enquire if there had been other offspring who were now deceased to account for the ten-year gap between Henry and herself. He was approaching his ninth birthday, the twins, Jonathan and Peter were almost seven and the baby of the family, Sarah, would be three next month.

She rather liked being an older sister and being able to assist in the children's upbringing. Papa was educating Henry whilst she acted as governess to the twins. There were not sufficient funds to employ anyone to do this task but she was more than happy to fulfil the role and put her excellent education to good use.

The journey was no more than a mile and could be accomplished in less than one half hour. There was only one thing she liked better than striding around the countryside enjoying the fresh air, and that was riding. Unfortunately, the only equine member of the family was an ancient cob used by her father on his parish visits so she was obliged to borrow a mount from her uncle if she wished to go out with her cousin.

Lady Patience, as her cousin was known by all except her own family, visited the rectory as often as Charity visited Bromley Hall. However, Patience always arrived accompanied by her personal maid and a footman, if she deigned to walk. Usually she would come on horseback or in a closed carriage. Their circumstances could not be more different, but they were as close as sisters being almost identical in looks and age. Indeed, strangers might take them for twins so alike were they.

Charity approached the magnificent edifice via the tradesman's entrance — this track took a more direct route to the side door which she always used. Not pausing to knock — there was no need as it was always open — she stepped into the spacious passageway pleased to be out of the chill February wind.

A footman arrived at her side, bowed politely and held out his hand to take her cloak and bonnet. 'Is Lady Patience in her apartment?'

'Her ladyship is in the Yellow Drawing Room, Miss Lawson. Do you wish me to announce you?'

She shook her head. 'No, I shall make my own way there.'

The drawing room was at the rear of the house and overlooked the park. The family used this smaller, more intimate chamber unless there were guests. She smiled; she was one of the family so didn't count. The double doors were open and the noise of children playing echoed down the corridor. Her Aunt Faith was rather lackadaisical about the rearing of her numerous children. They were rarely in the nursery or attending lessons in the schoolroom, but gadding about the place pursued by a variety of nursemaids and footmen.

The youngest set of twins, Mary Beth and Sarah Jane, who had recently celebrated their fifth name day, saw her first. 'It's Charity, Mama. She has a red face and mud on her skirts,' Sarah Jane announced with glee.

'Good morning, cousins, I've come to see your big sister. Can you spare her for a while?' She bent down and embraced both children warmly.

Aunt Faith was sitting on a *chaise longue* and waved her hand in greeting. 'Welcome, my dear, you have my permission to take Patience away. She has been entertaining my brood with a lively game of hunt the thimble. She deserves to escape for an hour or two.'

There was a chorus of disapproval from the four boys, but this was ignored. 'Thank goodness you have come to see me, Charity. I am quite exhausted. Behave yourselves, children, or Mama will send you back to the nursery.'

The two nursemaids in attendance immediately stepped forward and took over the game. The three sets of twins promptly transferred their attention and she and her cousin were able to escape without further comment.

'Come upstairs immediately, Charity, I have something of the utmost importance to tell you. In fact, I intended to visit you this afternoon if you hadn't come this morning.'

Intrigued by this remark, she readily followed up the handsome carved oak staircase, along the wide passageway to the west side of the building where Patience had her spacious apartment. As always she enjoyed the luxury of the fittings and furniture but she was not envious — she was perfectly content with her own lot in life and didn't yearn to be her cousin.

'Quickly, come and sit down on the window seat where we won't be overheard,' Patience said.

Oh dear! This wasn't going to be the usual *badinage*, but something far more serious. Much as she loved her flighty cousin she did sometimes wish that her overindulgent parents would take her in hand. The earl was rarely seen by anyone apart from his immediate family; he was obsessed with things scientifical and convinced he was going to discover some great secret he could share with the world.

Aunt Faith was equally reluctant to appear at society events and much preferred to recline on the sofa and spoil her many children. Her own mama was equally indolent when it came to discipline and etiquette — she supposed that as identical twins it was only to be expected the sisters were so similar. Indeed, they had produced daughters within days of each other and named them after virtues — as they themselves had been named.

She curled up beside her friend and waited to hear what madcap scheme Patience had become embroiled in this time. 'Well, my love, what's getting you in such a pother this morning?'

'I am in love with the most wonderful gentleman but I fear Papa might not quite like my choice.'

'In love? How can that be? When I saw you the day before yesterday you made no mention of it.'

Patience blushed and looked uncomfortable. 'I have been meeting him most afternoons for the past four days. I was out riding one day and we met at the ford. I was able to warn him not to attempt the crossing at it is far too deep in the winter.'

'That's all very well, but who is he? You cannot possibly be in love with someone you have only known for a few days.'

'His name is Jonathan Pettigrew, his father is Sir John Pettigrew and he is the heir.' She frowned and shook her head making her golden ringlets dance. 'I am not exactly sure where his estate might be, but I believe he mentioned it might be in Hertfordshire somewhere.'

The more she heard about this mysterious gentleman the more worried she was. 'If he hails from Hertfordshire what is he doing in Essex?'

'He is visiting an ancient relative in the neighbourhood; I've no idea who it is. Anyway, that is beside the point. Mr Pettigrew will be in London for the Season and I intend to be there as well. Now do you understand?'

'I'm totally at a loss. I understood that you were not to go to London this year as your parents have no wish for you to be married until you are of age.'

Patience grabbed her hands and

squeezed hard. 'Papa has a cousin who is married to a lord and has offered to present me — if you were to come too I believe I might persuade him that we are going to enjoy the parties and balls and not look for a husband.'

'I couldn't possibly go with you as I am needed at home. Also, we do not have the wherewithal to purchase me the necessary wardrobe — '

'Fiddlesticks to that! Do not you remember me telling you that my godmother has offered to pay for both of us? We are to reside with her. She is not prepared to accompany us to events, but we will be well-chaperoned by her ladyship.'

Charity sighed. 'That was indeed kind of her, but it doesn't solve the problem of my being essential for the smooth running of our household. We do not have a retinue of willing servants who can assist with the day-to-day duties. I cannot leave Mama to cope with the children on her own.'

Her cousin tumbled off the window

seat and without a word ran across the room and out of the door. What now? Should she follow her or remain where she was until Patience returned? The room was delightfully warm, unlike most of the chambers at the rectory, and even sitting so far from the fire she was quite warm.

The door from the bedchamber swung open and two smiling parlour-maids walked in carrying refreshments. Despite having eaten a hearty breakfast an hour or so ago the smell of the freshly baked scones and a jug of chocolate made her stomach rumble.

'How delicious, please put the trays on the bureau. Lady Patience is elsewhere, but I am sure she will return at any moment.'

The girls curtsied and whisked out of the door. Should she help herself or wait until her cousin rejoined her? She strolled across to examine the contents of the trays — not only were there scones, butter and strawberry conserve but also slices of plum cake, cold cuts and chutney, plus fresh bread. This was a veritable feast which would set her up nicely before her walk back across the fields.

As she was pondering her cousin burst back into the room. 'There, it is all arranged. Mama has agreed to send two nursemaids to help whilst you're away. Letters have been sent to London and we shall depart in two days' time. As you don't have your own abigail Mama suggests you borrow a girl from here. Anna, my dresser, will know who to choose.'

'Am I to have no say in the matter? You know I am not comfortable at grand events and the thought of parading in front of strangers fills me with trepidation.'

'I have thought of that, and whilst our new gowns are being made up we shall employ a dance master so we will be proficient when the Season starts in full. I expect it will take a few weeks to complete our clothes, more than enough time for you to become familiar with London.' Her cousin realised she was not convinced. 'We can visit all the sights, go to Hatchards and purchase the latest novels, see the menagerie at the Tower and no doubt there will be several boring lectures you can attend as well.'

'I would dearly like to go to the opera and theatre — if you promise me we can do that then I shall be more than delighted to accompany you. However, you must give me your word you will not attempt to meet Mr Pettigrew in secret.'

Patience clapped her hands and twirled around the room. 'I promise. Oh, we shall have such fun, we do not have to attend Almack's where Mama says all the hopeful debutantes must go in order to search for husbands. I believe that the supper is indifferent and the ladies who run the place are veritable dragons.'

'In which case, I am thoroughly relieved we do not have to go there. Do you mind if I help myself to this delicious repast? I am decidedly hungry.'

By the time the trays were empty she was eagerly anticipating her visit to the capital. She pushed aside her worries about Mr Pettigrew, time enough to intervene when they were actually in Town. She was brushing crumbs from her skirt when her aunt strolled in waving a note.

'Charity, my love, your papa has given his consent to you accompanying Patience. There is one thing I need to make clear to you both, whilst you are residing under Lady Harriet's roof, her nephew will be *in loco parentis*. We would not be comfortable without a suitable guardian in place.'

Her cousin looked horrified but Charity was delighted there would be someone in authority and it would not be entirely down to her to keep her wayward cousin in line.

Her aunt smiled at her daughter. 'I must remind you, Patience, my dearest one, that with your pedigree and substantial dowry you will be the target of unscrupulous fortune hunters. I am relying on your cousin to ensure that you do nothing foolish. Do you give me your word, both of you, that you will behave with the utmost decorum whilst you are in Town?'

'I do indeed, Aunt Faith, the last thing on our minds will be eligible gentlemen. Mind you, I doubt that anyone eligible would be interested in an impecunious daughter of a local rector.'

'You are a remarkably pretty young lady, I'm sure there is a gentleman somewhere who would be prepared to marry a girl like you.' Her aunt smiled vaguely and sailed out of the room apparently unaware that her daughter had failed to give the required promise.

Charity waited until the door was closed before speaking her mind. 'I wish to make one thing abundantly clear; I will not be inveigled into deception of any sort, Patience. I repeat, that you must forget any notion of secret assignations with this mysterious Mr Pettigrew

— I shall not hesitate to inform our temporary guardian if you attempt to meet him.' She hoped her stern words would be enough to persuade her cousin not to pursue this infatuation.

★   ★   ★

Two days later she left her familial home to spend four months in the capital pretending to be something she was not. There was not a drop of aristocratic blood in her veins — unlike her cousin. She hoped one day to meet a young man who might suit her as a husband, perhaps a farmer or a schoolmaster, or maybe a man of the cloth like her own dear father. Of course, if the son of the local squire should turn out to be available and to her liking he would be ideal.

Her aunt had captured the heart of the earl at the local assembly — she had not needed a London Season to make a brilliant match. Mama had settled for Papa and had never felt a moment's

16

regret or wished to exchange places with her more fortunate sister.

Patience had a head filled with flummery, but she had not a romantic bone in her body. She thought love all very well in novels but not at all practical in real life. Far better to base a relationship on compatibility, respect and affection, for this was likely to stand the test of time, unlike something based on physical attraction.

'I do not like travelling long distances, Charity, but this is one occasion when I will endure as I do so wish to go to London.'

'I have never travelled more than a few miles in my entire life, I have no idea how I will react to a journey of three hours. By the by, I must thank you for giving me these smart clothes.'

'Mama insisted, she said she did not want her favourite niece looking like a poor relation — '

Charity giggled. 'Even though I am exactly that? Anyway, I have never owned anything so grand.' When the outfits had arrived the previous day she had opened the box with trepidation. Her cousin favoured frills and furbelows and she preferred her gowns to be plain. However, the ensembles were perfect. She particularly liked this travelling gown in dark blue with a matching cloak and bonnet.

'I have never worn them, they are not to my taste, so you are doing me a favour by accepting them. Papa cannot complain that he has wasted money on clothes that will never be worn.'

'I cannot believe we are to have more new gowns. Whatever will I do with them when I return? I cannot lord it over Mama dressed like a lady of means.'

'I am sure she will be delighted to see you looking smart. I overheard her talking to Mama not long ago saying that she wished your papa was not so proud and would accept help.'

'Then, dearest cousin, I am doubly delighted to be so well turned out. I'm also pleased that our maids travelled ahead of us and we have the carriage to ourselves for there is something most particular I wish to say to you . . . '

Her cousin waved an airy hand. 'Fiddlesticks to that! You have already made your opinion quite clear, there is no need to repeat yourself. I have quite forgotten about that gentleman, I can assure you. Meeting him was the impetus I needed to ask to attend a Season, no more than that. I cannot tell you how excited I am at the thought of attending soirées, balls and musicales.'

'In which case, my love, I shall say no more on the subject. I am dreading what you are looking forward to, but cannot wait to enjoy what London has to offer.'

The carriage lapsed into silence and her cousin dozed whilst she gazed wide-eyed out of the window at the ever-changing scenery. Eventually she too fell asleep only to be wakened by her cousin's complaint.

'This journey is beyond tedious, Charity, I swear that every part of my anatomy is bruised or damaged after spending so long in this infernal carriage.'

'Good grief, dearest one, we have scarcely been travelling for three hours and should arrive at our destination very shortly. Have you not looked out of the window and seen that we are now progressing through the city of London? I believe St Paul's Cathedral to be in this vicinity.'

Her cousin shrugged. 'I care not for such things. Tell me again where we are to reside.'

'A house in Hanover Square, I believe that to be a pleasant part of Town. I am intending to take long walks and if there is a suitable horse, to ride in Hyde Park or Green Park.'

Patience yawned. 'As long as you do not expect me to accompany you, I wish you well of your intentions.'

Less than twenty minutes later the vehicle rocked to a standstill outside an imposing building. There were scrubbed stone steps leading up to a handsome door with a brass knocker. Before the steps were let down the front door was opened and a veritable army of footmen emerged.

Charity sat back on the squabs. 'Who is your godmother, Patience? She must be wealthy indeed to employ so many indoor staff. I'd hoped we were to stay somewhere less ostentatious for I fear I shall be sadly out of my depth here.'

The carriage door was opened before she received an answer. Her cousin allowed herself to be handed out and Charity copied her actions. A middle-aged gentleman attired entirely in black was waiting to bow them in. 'My lady, Miss Lawson, welcome to Hawkridge House. His Grace The Duke of Edbury will see you in the drawing room at midday. Mrs Burson, the housekeeper, will show you to your apartments.'

2

'Aunt Harry, I cannot imagine why I allowed myself to be talked into this nonsense. Escorting two provincial misses about the place will surely engender a deal of speculative comment?' Hugo had seen the smart travelling carriage arrive outside the house.

'My dear boy, when your parents died from typhus ten years ago I vowed to do what I could to see you happily established. I have watched you expertly evade a variety of hopeful young ladies but the time has come for you to find yourself a suitable wife.'

He raised an eyebrow. 'And you think that one of these schoolroom chits will suit me? Why is that, I wonder?' He strolled away from the window and took the armchair opposite his last remaining relative.

'Good heavens, Hugo, I would not

dream of suggesting you take an interest in Miss Lawson, she would not do at all. However, my goddaughter, Lady Patience, is another matter altogether. She is impeccably bred — unfortunately only on her father's side — and has a very substantial dowry. She is also a pretty little thing and will be easily guided.'

'You appear to have it all worked out. I could certainly use some extra funds as my dear departed father made sure my inheritance had been spent before he died. Even after my economies and selling a substantial amount of land, I am still struggling to keep Edbury afloat.' He rubbed his eyes and felt the weight of his responsibilities bowing him down. 'If I'm not to lose everything I must marry money.'

'It is a great shame, my boy, that you did not take the plunge several years ago but have left matters until they have become so dire you have no choice. However, I shall say no more on the subject. I am sure that my goddaughter is the right choice for you. That is why I asked you to stand as their guardian whilst they are staying here. It will give you ample time to get to know the girl and see if you will suit.'

He chuckled. 'I sincerely hope the young lady in question is not aware of your motive for inviting her here for the Season. I shall not offer for her if I don't think we are compatible and I have no wish to cause her embarrassment.'

'I am not a pea goose, I would not dream of putting either of you in such an invidious position. You may rest assured the last thing on the child's mind is matrimony. In fact the earl was quite specific in his instructions. His daughter is not to attend Almack's and you are to make clear to any would-be suitors that she is not on the marriage mart. He does not wish her to embark on matrimony until she is one and twenty — another two years. She has come to enjoy the parties — nothing more.'

'Good God! I am to keep Lady Patience safe from predatory males whilst pursuing her for myself?' He jumped to his feet and began to stride about the room. 'I'm not happy with this, Aunt Harry. I have no wish to be part of such a deception. I am withdrawing my offer and you will have to find yourself another temporary guardian for your girls.'

'For heaven's sake, Hugo, do not get onto your high horse. You will not be pursuing the girl, merely getting to know her with no formal expectations on either side. If you believe she will make you a suitable bride then you can go and see her parents.' Rather than looking dismayed by his outburst she was smiling. 'Please sit down again and stop perambulating about the room like a caged tiger. Do you honestly think any parent is going to turn down an offer from a duke — even one as impecunious as you?'

She was right of course, a duke of any sort, however old or strapped for cash, would be on the top of the list for all matrons seeking husbands for their hopeful daughters. He subsided into the chair and grinned.

'I beg your pardon for being so curmudgeonly. As you know I abhor any kind of deceit. Mama was devastated when she discovered my father had a mistress and several by-blows and had gambled away everything.'

'That is water under the bridge, my boy, high time you put it to one side and got on with your own life. You are not your father, you have not a deceitful bone in your body and won't take advantage of the situation.'

The die was cast, he was committed and for the first time in many years he could see light at the end of the tunnel. He hoped Lady Patience might be the answer to his prayers.

★ ★ ★

Patience grabbed Charity's elbow and she flinched at the grip. 'Quickly, we mustn't be seen. Come upstairs, there's something I must tell you.'

As they were already on their way she couldn't understand her cousin's anxiety. 'I'm coming, and as far as I can see we are not observed by anyone apart from the staff.' This conversation was being conducted in a whisper. Burson walked stiff-backed ahead of them. Neither she nor the butler had seemed particularly friendly. She was used to accommodating servants, not those who looked down their noses at one.

'Burson, I require the name of the butler. I also wish to have a footman delegated to escorting us on our promenades. I also wish to ride before breakfast every morning — kindly ensure there is a groom and a suitable mount waiting for me.'

Patience looked astonished, and well might her cousin do so, for she was not famous for making demands and especially in such an imperious manner. She grinned and put her finger to her lips and waited for the housekeeper to turn and speak — which she did with alacrity.

'I beg your pardon, my lady, for not informing you. The butler is Mr Reynolds and he will assign a member of staff for your convenience. I will pass on your request to the stable. Lady Harriet was most insistent that you are to have anything you ask for.'

'I am delighted to hear you say so, for I was not impressed with the reception we received. No doubt things will improve from this point forward.' Charity nodded regally, barely able to keep back her giggles at the charade they were enacting.

The housekeeper curtsied and led them to a delightful apartment at the rear of the building which overlooked the substantial garden. 'Lady Harriet thought that you would wish to share with your cousin, but if this is not to your liking, we can move Miss Lawson to an adjacent apartment.'

'We are happy to share. That will be all, Burson.' Her cousin was all but vibrating beside her in an effort to keep back her laughter — the sooner the housekeeper left, the better.

When the door closed they fell into each other's arms laughing helplessly. After a few moments Charity recovered her composure. 'I shouldn't have done that, Patience, but the woman was so unpleasant I couldn't resist. I'm sorry she mistook me for you, it was certainly not my intention.'

Instead of being outraged at the deception, her cousin clapped her hands. 'I would never have suggested it, but now it has happened, I beg you to maintain the masquerade. I shall be able to enjoy myself without fear of being pursued by hopeful husbands. You can enjoy yourself knowing that you too are safe from entanglement as you are not who you are pretending to be.'

'Put that way, my love, I can see the advantages. But surely your godmother will know at once that I am not you — although we could be sisters — twins even — my hair does not fall into ringlets and my eyes are not the same shade of blue.'

'I have not met Lady Harriet since I was an infant in leading strings, she does not come to the country and we do not go to Town. You know as much about me and my family as I do so I cannot see a problem there.'

'The only snag in this arrangement is that I wish to visit the sights and you do not.'

'As far as I am aware my godmother has no idea of my tastes. We shall continue to behave as we've always done only you shall answer to my name and I to yours.' She pursed her lips. 'However, I do recall that Mama mentioned I was a girl with no interest in anything apart from fashion and parties.'

'In which case our scheme is doomed to failure for I refuse point blank to become frivolous.'

'And I have no intention of becoming a bluestocking. How shall we resolve this?'

'I think it best that we resume our natural places in society. As you know, I'm not comfortable with any sort of deception and although this is purely for our own amusement, I should much prefer to remain Miss Lawson.'

Patience shook her head. 'Please, cousin, let us do it until we are discovered. We shall behave as usual, and when Lady Harriet comments on my change of character we can explain we have been having fun. That Burson made the mistake and we decided to continue with the joke.'

'Very well, under those conditions I reluctantly agree. In fact, I'm looking forward to playing the trick on our temporary guardian. Imagine having a duke of the realm at our beck and call — no doubt he is full of his own importance as such men are, and will treat you as if you are of no account.'

She glanced at the mantel clock and saw to her horror there was scarcely half an hour until they were to present themselves in the drawing room.

'We must get changed at once, Patience. Also, Anna and the other girl must be informed of our deception.'

'I forgot to tell you, Anna had the measles and could not accompany us. We have two maids I scarcely know to take care of us. They will accept us in our new personas without question.'

* * *

In less than the allotted time they were in fresh gowns. 'I still think that you should have worn my choice, Charity, I cannot believe my godmother will not immediately see that we are dissembling. A flighty young lady would not wear such a plain gown.'

'My ensemble is made of the finest jaconet muslin and trimmed at the throat with exquisite Brussels lace. The forget-me-not blue is exactly the shade of my eyes and I think I look every inch an aristocrat.' She straightened her shoulders, looked suitably disdainful and strolled across the sitting room much to the amusement of her companion.

'My gown has only three frills at the hem and I do declare that rose silk is the perfect complement to my ringlets and sky-blue eyes.' Her cousin fluttered her long, dark eyelashes — another feature that they shared — and minced across the room with a decidedly silly expression.

'We must go down — I have decided we shall let fate determine whether we continue with this joke. Neither of us will speak, we must curtsy politely and wait and see how we are addressed. Do you agree, Patience?'

'I do. Then they can only blame themselves if they have confused us. When I suggested this visit I had no idea what fun it was going to be.'

They rushed from the room arm and arm almost colliding with a personable young footman who bowed. 'My lady, Miss Lawson, I am to conduct you to the Grand Drawing Room.'

Charity was tempted to ask his name,

but recalled that her aunt had once told her you never made small talk with servants. It was their duty to recognise you but you were not obliged to do the same.

She exchanged a smile with her cousin and they glided elegantly along the spacious passageway and down the staircase. The vast, black and white chequered vestibule would have comfortably accommodated the entire rectory. There was no sign of the butler but there were two bewigged footmen standing by the double doors waiting to fling them open.

Now the time had come she was bitterly regretting their decision to go along with this impersonation. In her limited experience subterfuge of any description rarely led to a happy outcome. Too late to repine — she was committed.

Her cousin seemed to be suffering no such anxieties of conscience. Her hand was relaxed as was her demeanour — in fact Patience seemed to be enjoying it far too much. But then she was the one for play-acting and theatricals and always dragged her complaining siblings into performing in front of their guests at the Christmas festivities.

Their tame footman ignored those who had opened the doors and stepped forward to announce loudly, 'Lady Patience and Miss Lawson, my lady and your grace.'

He stepped to one side and she was propelled forward by her cousin's vice-like grip on her arm. She didn't dare to raise her eyes, was sure guilt would be written clearly on her face, but sank into a graceful curtsy with perfect synchronicity with her cousin.

They straightened together. The silence stretched. This wasn't going to work — one of them had better announce their identity before the situation descended into farce. She glanced at her companion and together they raised their heads and stepped apart.

'Patience, my dear, you are exactly as I imagined you. Miss Lawson, welcome to my home. Might I introduce you to my nephew, His Grace The Duke of Edbury.'

The moment had come when they must reveal their true identities or continue the deception. The duke was on his feet. He was a prodigious height, he must be more than two yards tall. He wore his dark hair unfashionably long, and tied at the nape of his neck with a black ribbon. He was dressed casually. He didn't wear a close-fitting jacket from Westons nor calfskin breeches, but garments more suited to a country squire than a toplofty aristocrat.

He bowed to her cousin. 'I'm delighted to meet you, Miss Lawson, I hope you enjoy your stay.' He turned to her and bowed again, no lower nor with more aplomb than he had done before. 'Lady Patience, I have heard much about you from my aunt and look forward to furthering our acquaintance.'

Now was the time to disabuse them, to laugh gaily at the error, before they became too deeply embroiled. She drew breath to correct his assumption but her cousin forestalled her.

'Your grace, Patience and I are thrilled to be here and cannot wait to visit the sights and attend the opera and theatre.'

He smiled and gestured to a silk-covered *chaise longue*. 'Won't you be seated?'

There was no opportunity to stop this progressing as Patience was ignoring her. She had to say something — she was in danger of appearing a simpleton. Before she could speak the duke addressed her directly.

'I gather you are a keen horsewoman, my lady. I shall join you. Will seven o'clock tomorrow morning be suitable?'

'It will, your grace. I hope there is another mount for my cousin as she too likes to ride when she has the opportunity.'

Patience patted her arm rather harder than was necessary. 'I have not ridden for a while so would only hold up such experienced riders. Perhaps another time?'

This was making matters so much worse. Now Lady Harriet and her nephew believed she was the accomplished equestrian — she would be given a horse she couldn't control and make a ninny of herself.

'Of course, I will ensure there is a quiet mare for you to use. I understand from my aunt that you cannot be seen in public until you have replenished your wardrobes. I gather the mantua-maker is due soon so I will take my leave.'

Charity was a trifle startled by his casual comment which implied they were inappropriately dressed, then he caught her eye and raised a finely arched, dark eyebrow. He was poking fun at her aunt and sharing his jest with her. She returned his gesture with a half-smile, unaccountably flustered by his attention — and he did have the most unusual eyes, so dark they were almost black.

She and Patience stood politely — after all he was a duke and their temporary guardian. He nodded and strolled out — the room seemed strangely flat without him.

3

The afternoon passed in a flurry of measuring and materials — by the time the seamstresses had departed Charity was exhausted.

'I cannot imagine we will ever wear everything we've ordered.' She flopped down on the sofa and her cousin joined her. 'I notice that your choices were almost identical to mine. I have asked for more decoration and you have asked for less. In fact, dearest, when we have our new wardrobe, we could wear each other's gowns without complaint.'

'Shall we have done and arrange them in one closet? Then we can wear whatever we fancy.' Patience giggled and tucked her feet under her. 'We will confuse the duke and his aunt even more by doing this.'

'There is one aspect of this escapade

we had not thought out properly. How are we to address each other in private?'

'There's no need to use either name, thus we will prevent any errors.'

'I have no wish to change yet again and go down to dinner tonight. I would like to ask for a tray to be brought up, are you happy for me to do so?'

Her cousin nodded. 'I never thought I could be exhausted selecting new gowns, but I own I am quite fatigued. Remember, we have travelled from Essex today as well as having the excitement of meeting a genuine duke *and* my godmother. Please, arrange for our supper to be brought to us here.'

Charity retired at eight o'clock, relieved she did not have to share a bed even though she was sharing the apartment. There were two large, canopied beds in the bedchamber and there was still room to dance a minuet if one so wished. She had asked for a habit to be put out in the dressing room for her ride the next morning, but had told the maids she had no need of their assistance so early.

The room was dark when she woke, she had no idea of the time, but her body clock told her she had been at her slumbers long enough. Her cousin was sleeping soundly on the other side of the room. There was sufficient light from the embers of the fire to allow her to cross the room safely and enter the substantial dressing room.

She discovered a taper on the shelf and pushed it into the fire, relieved when it caught light immediately. There were candlesticks waiting and she soon had the room bathed in a golden, flickering glow. A spectacular blue velvet riding habit had been set out for her. She was almost dazzled by the gold buttons and frogging on the shoulders. It had been made to ape the military style and there was even a smart blue cap to complete the ensemble. She smiled as she dressed — in this outfit no one would mistake her for Miss Lawson. She prayed she would not frighten the horses with her magnificence.

As she crept from the sitting room a further problem presented itself. So early in the morning their tame footman would not be on guard outside and she would have to find her own way through this vast establishment and then to the stable yard.

She had checked the clock and knew the time to be just after six thirty — she had no wish to be late for her appointment. The one good thing about her startling appearance was that the duke would be so bedazzled (or horrified) he would scarcely pay her any attention.

The wall sconces were still flickering — no expense was spared here if these were left burning all night. She was grateful there had been no necessity to bring a heavy silver candlestick with her. Finding her way to the vestibule was comparatively easy as she had a reasonable sense of direction. However, when faced with five passageways leading off in different directions she had no notion which one to choose.

She closed her eyes and imagined herself outside the house. Yes — the archway that led to the coach house and stables had been to the left, so presumably any exit on the west side of the house would take her in the right direction.

She was still hesitating when there was the sound of female voices approaching. Four housemaids emerged from the smallest passageway carrying pails and mops.

On seeing her they huddled together clucking and muttering like a flock of chickens in a farmyard.

'Good morning, I wish to go to the stables; kindly direct me to the correct entrance.'

One of the group shoved her bucket and mop into the hands of the girl beside her and stepped forward. Her voluminous calico apron and unattractive cap made her indistinguishable from her peers. The girl curtsied. 'I'll show you, my lady, you will likely get lost if I ain't with you.'

Charity sailed past the others and

followed the girl down the corridor from which the maids had emerged. She was obviously being taken via the servants' route, no doubt quicker and possibly the only one the housemaid knew.

Although the wall sconces were not as frequent here, they were still alight. Even the servants didn't have to carry candlesticks around with them. Such luxury! She could become accustomed to living so well and might not wish to return to her simple lifestyle at the rectory.

She hid her smile behind her hand. How strange, her play-acting was beginning to take over her common sense. She would hate to live surrounded by minions, unable to do anything for herself. She much preferred the freedom of her current existence, however simple her lifestyle.

The girl skidded to a halt at a side door which was already unbolted. 'If you go out there, my lady, you'll be in the kitchen yard. Take the path to the left and go through the arch and you'll be able to see the stable yard.' The girl bobbed again and scurried back down the passageway leaving Charity to open the door herself.

Obviously, not everybody thought her incapable of opening a door. She stepped into the cold, early morning darkness and shivered. Although it was barely light enough to see, she had no difficulty finding the direction as the clatter of ironshod hoofs was clearly audible.

There were no horses saddled and waiting, but then there was still half an hour to the appointed time. A smartly dressed man in a tweed jacket, buff breeches and cap came towards her and bowed.

'Good morning, my lady. I hoped you was coming a bit early so you can choose your own ride.'

'I would like to do so — perhaps you could show me what you have to offer?'

The second box held exactly the right mount for her — a moderate-sized bay gelding with kind eyes and gentle spirit.

'This one, if you please. What is his name?'

'Trojan, my lady. He's a gentleman, goes well under side-saddle, and will cause you no problems.'

'I decided a quiet mount would be better for someone not accustomed to London traffic.' There was no sign of the duke and on impulse she decided not to wait. 'I shall go out immediately. Let his grace know my direction.' The head groom looked puzzled, as well he might. 'I assume the groom will know where best to guide me?'

'Yes, my lady. Green Park is quiet this time of the morning.'

Soon she was in the saddle, her skirts adjusted, and ready to depart. Trojan stood quietly and the groom, riding a handsome chestnut, led the way from the yard, under the arch and into a deserted street. There was sufficient light to see, but the sun was yet to rise. Was she foolhardy to venture out before dawn in February?

The groom turned in his saddle to

speak to her. 'No frost this morning, my lady, be safe enough for a grand gallop.'

Charity shuddered. 'Excellent, I shall take your lead.'

She wondered how she would have fared if the streets had been filled with the usual carriages, diligences, carts and such like. Her horse was well-mannered and obedient to bit and heel — she was fairly sure he would not jibe or shy if something untoward were to happen. However, riding on cobbled streets was not the same as riding in the open country. If she took a tumble here she would probably break a bone, or worse.

*　　*　　*

Hugo swore at his valet — and the poor man dropped the shaving water. 'I apologise, Jenkins, I am in a hurry this morning and this is making me tetchy.' This statement caused his man to shake his head violently — a difficult task when attempting to refill the shaving bowl.

'Your grace, I was clumsy, please forgive *me*. We will be done in a few minutes.'

No sooner was he shaved than Hugo rammed his arms into his riding coat, grabbed his gloves and beaver, and strode from the room. He heard the tall clock in the vestibule strike the hour — tarnation take it — he would be unpardonably late.

He took the stairs two at a time and was out of the house in moments. His stallion was stamping impatiently in the yard, swinging the stableboy into the air each time he plunged.

'I apologise for keeping you waiting, Tom, I hope Sinbad has not crushed your toes this morning.'

The boy grinned and tossed the reins over. 'No, your grace, not today. I reckon we're getting to understand each other a mite better.'

Hugo vaulted into the saddle, shoved his feet into the irons and clicked his tongue. Sinbad shot forward, almost unseating him, and he swore again. It took him several minutes to settle his volatile mount; he had scared a flock of pigeons and two servant girls scrubbing a flight of steps before the animal stopped his antics.

His mouth curved into a rueful smile. He considered himself a relaxed and jovial sort of fellow, not one to stand on ceremony or treat his staff unfairly, but this morning he had sworn at poor Jenkins and quite upset the man. What was the matter with him? Surely it wasn't the prospect of entering parson's mousetrap that was causing his uncharacteristic choler?

This thought turned his mind to the girl Aunt Harry thought a suitable bride for him. She was comely, tall but with womanly curves, pretty corn-coloured hair and sparkling blue eyes — indeed, both she and her cousin were diamonds of the first water. If he had to marry an heiress, which he did, then Lady Patience might well be the perfect choice.

He pushed his mount into an

extended trot and arrived in Hanover Square barely fifteen minutes late. He was astonished to discover that not only had the girl not had the courtesy to wait for him, but had actually set off on her own fifteen minutes before the agreed time to meet. He was unused to being treated with such disrespect and had every intention of taking the girl to task.

She was heading for Green Park; he should be able to catch her up before she got there if he hurried.

★ ★ ★

By the time Charity arrived at the park gates there was a watery sun to light her way. Even with the trees bare the place looked inviting. She had forgotten she was to ride with the duke and urged her mount next to the groom. 'I shall canter around the perimeter and if the park is still deserted then I might indeed gallop.' No young lady would dream of galloping in public — not if she wished to keep her reputation.

'No one here so early, my lady. You go at your own pace, we'll keep behind you.'

Trojan pricked his ears and danced sideways in his eagerness to stretch his legs. 'Alright, my boy, we shall take it slowly for the first mile and then you can gallop.'

She settled into the saddle and tapped the horse's side with her heel. He sprung into a canter from a standstill and she was glad she had a firm hold or she would have flown over his head. The naked trees became a blur and for a horrible moment she thought she was losing control — then she relaxed and so did Trojan. His long-strided canter was comfortable and he showed no inclination to take the bit, and bolt.

She decided it would be foolish to gallop on her first ride for many weeks so reined back as she reached the end of the first track. Her horse was scarcely blowing and she leant forward to pat his neck. As she did so something caught her eye. Beneath the trees a few hundred yards away was what looked like a pile of rags. When she sat up she could no longer see it — she was intrigued.

Her groom pulled up beside her. 'I'm going to ride over there; I shall be out of sight, but within earshot. I wish you to remain here in case his grace arrives. Kindly direct him to me if he comes before I return.'

What he thought of her request she didn't remain long enough to ascertain. She leaned down a second time to make sure she was riding in the correct direction. Yes — the bundle of cloth was there. In order to reach it she had to dismount and tie her horse to a convenient branch. She had travelled only a short distance into the thicket when she heard a plaintive wail.

Her stomach somersaulted. She recognised that sound. The poor little thing had spent the night outside — it was a miracle the infant had survived. She dropped to her knees, heedless of the damage she was doing to her cousin's habit, and forced her way into the centre of the undergrowth. As she reached the bundle it moved and two chubby arms waved in the air. The plaintive screams redoubled now that a rescue was at hand.

'Good morning, little one. I am here to take you home. Come along, I shall wrap you in my skirt.' She unbuttoned this without hesitation and stood in her breeches and boots. It was harder than she'd expected to gather up the baby and envelop him in her habit. He was surprisingly heavy and decidedly smelly, and not a newborn as she'd expected, but an infant of at least nine months.

He continued to cry but with less gusto than before as she slowly edged backwards with the precious baby in her arms. She continued to talk softly to him and his sobs became sniffles and then he was quiet. Having taken care of her younger siblings over the years she was familiar with babies and was not perturbed by his silence. The child was asleep — exhausted by his crying and able to rest now he was safe and warm.

Trojan was standing patiently where she'd left him. 'Good fellow, I'm so pleased you are still here.' She could not attempt to remount holding the child so must find the groom. Should she shout for aid or wait until the man arrived?

The gelding turned his head and whickered. Someone was coming. Thank goodness — the groom had arrived to see what was keeping her. 'I'm here. You must help me at once,' she yelled, causing the gelding to shy sideways.

From around the corner came the duke. He stared down at her and did not seem particularly impressed by what he saw — in fact his expression was stern and not at all encouraging.

4

Charity decided to address him before he could admonish her. 'Your grace, thank goodness you are here. I have found a baby abandoned under the bushes — I fear for his health if he is not immediately taken somewhere warm.'

Instantly his demeanour changed, and without hesitation he dropped to the ground and stripped off his fine jacket. 'Here, my dear, hand the infant to me and you can replace your skirt.'

Only then did she understand the enormity of her actions. Small wonder he had been looking shocked — a well brought up young lady should never be seen without her skirt, even if she was decently attired in breeches. She held out her arms and he gently plucked the sleeping child from the cocoon of her habit. He politely turned his back whilst she deftly buttoned herself in.

'Do you wish me to carry the baby or shall I attempt to remount?' She expected him to immediately thrust the child into her arms, but he shook his head.

'I can manage, if you can do the same.'

The problem was solved as the groom trotted up and could toss her into the saddle. 'If you are ready, my lady, we must make haste. This little one has been outside for far too long.' The duke turned to the groom, who had remounted. 'Ride ahead to my house in St James's Square — do you know the direction?' The man nodded. 'Then go for the doctor yourself. My housekeeper will know what to do, so make sure you give my message directly to her.'

Charity held out her arms and he passed the baby to her whilst he jumped into the saddle. 'Give him to me, my dear, he is too heavy for you to carry and ride safely.'

Obediently she handed the precious parcel to him and he tucked the baby under his arm as if he had been doing it every day of his life. He took the lead and she dropped in behind him as they cantered towards the gates. She could not help but notice the extraordinary breadth of his shoulders as these were even more noticeable without the camouflage of his jacket.

How many other gentlemen would have been happy to ruin their coat in such a way? Although she'd known him barely four and twenty hours, she was already coming to like him far too much. This would not do at all. When she returned she would insist that Patience give up the pretence and they resume their correct positions in society.

The streets were slightly more busy, but not enough traffic or noisy pedestrians to cause her any alarm. They did not canter over the cobbles but he kept his stallion in an extended walk the short distance to his town house. He turned immediately through an archway that led, in a similar fashion as the one in Hanover Square, to a busy stable yard.

There was a welcome committee waiting on the freshly swept cobbles. A smiling lady of middle years, dressed in smart blue bombazine, stood flanked by equally smart housemaids. They all curtsied. The housekeeper, for she could be none other, stepped forward with open arms.

'Let me take the infant, your grace, I have a warm bath ready and Cook is preparing milk and porridge.'

The duke handed down the baby and was on his feet before the woman had moved. 'I'm sure there is a crib somewhere in the attics, Garfield, which would be ideal.'

She nodded. 'It is already in the nursery, waiting. Although we have no trained nursery maids, your grace, these two girls have experience with infants and will make ideal carers.'

Charity slid to the ground unaided and was obliged to clutch the pommel to prevent her knees from buckling beneath her. Hastily she recovered her equilibrium, embarrassed to appear so feeble. She wasn't sure why she had come to his house, surely she should have returned as planned to Hanover Square?

'Your grace, as you have this situation firmly in hand, I shall return home. I have no wish to worry Lady Harriet.' She had been about to say her cousin's name but remembered just in time.

He smiled and a strange and unexpected warmth flooded through her. He really was a most attractive gentleman. 'I shall send a note explaining what has transpired, my dear, you look done in. I will not have you riding around the streets unescorted.'

She bristled. 'I wasn't intending to leave until my groom returned, your grace. I am not a widgeon.'

'I do not wish to stand bandying words with you in my stable yard.' His smile had gone but his eyes twinkled. He offered his arm and she had no option but to place her hand upon it.

'Also, my dear girl, your presence here is causing alarm amongst my horses. They are not accustomed to seeing such a spectacle here.'

'Are you suggesting my ensemble is not to your liking? I can assure you that the military style is all the rage at the moment.'

He chuckled and grinned down at her. 'How true, my dear, but you have enough gold on your habit to embellish a dozen such outfits.'

Her laughter echoed along the path. 'I cannot deny it. I know this to be a mistake — somehow my instructions to the mantua-maker were misunderstood.'

'I'm relieved to hear you say so for I could not help but wonder what you would appear in next. I take it you don't have another such ensemble to frighten my horses?'

They had now reached the side door which was standing open. She was surprised there were no flunkies waiting to bow them in as there were at

Hanover Square. He guided her down a passage and into a spacious entrance hall.

She was rather enjoying his company and waited expectantly to be invited to break her fast. Instead he curled his aristocratic nose and shook his head. 'You cannot remain in that skirt, my girl, from the aroma it must be liberally smeared with baby excrement.'

She recoiled, almost tripping over her skirts in her shock at his blunt comment. Then she saw he was laughing. 'Now that you come to mention it, your grace, I do smell rather distinctive. Am I to assume that you have something suitable I can change into?'

'My sister always leaves a variety of garments behind her when she has visited.' He narrowed his eyes and stared at her intently. 'I believe you to be of similar stature, I'm sure you will find something to your taste.' He half-bowed. 'Although you are too polite to mention it, I must also change my raiment. We will breakfast together in half an hour

— can you be ready by then?'

'I can be ready in half that time, but no doubt such an illustrious gentleman as yourself requires far longer.'

He smiled and strolled off into the depths of the house leaving her stranded with no idea where she should be going. He must have his rooms downstairs unless there were other ways of reaching the bedchambers. She could hardly wander from room to room searching for his sister's apartment. She looked around the vestibule but could see no bell to ring.

The housekeeper had taken the baby to the nursery, which must be on an upper floor. She would find her way there and then get the necessary directions. Now the matter had been drawn to her attention she was finding the noxious aroma extremely unpleasant. She was no longer in public so could see no harm in removing the offending garment and continuing in her perfectly decent breeches.

She rolled the skirt into a bundle and

placed it prominently in the centre of the hall. No doubt a servant would eventually come across it and take it to the laundry to be cleaned. Freed from the voluminous material, she scampered up the stairs and then searched for the second flight which should lead to the nursery floor. She discovered that and dashed up hoping she would find the housekeeper immediately, as she was determined to be downstairs within the allotted time.

She emerged on a sunny corridor and immediately heard voices coming from an open doorway. She walked in to discover the infant she and the duke had rescued, splashing in a bath.

'I'm sorry to disturb you, but could one of your girls take me to the chamber in which I shall find a gown I can change into?'

The housekeeper turned and instead of looking upset at this interruption she smiled. 'Just look at him, my lady, this is a healthy and happy infant. See how covered he is — he's been well tended up until last night.' She pointed to the clothes she'd removed from the baby. 'His gown is made from the finest cambric, the shawl of lamb's wool. This child comes from a well-to-do family, of that I'm sure.'

'You're quite right, which makes his abandonment even stranger. He is also not a newborn, I should think he is nine months at least.' She crouched down and took the baby's hand. He chuckled and splashed her. 'Well, little one, you are obviously contented now. The duke and I will endeavour to solve the puzzle and return you to your parents as soon as may be.'

One of the maids was hovering by the door waiting to escort her downstairs to the chamber she required. The girl remained to help her. Charity discarded her clothes, shivering as she did so, as there was no fire burning here. She spent a few moments on her ablutions, and then hastily stepped into the necessary underpinnings. She scarcely noticed the gown she stepped into as she was more concerned with being ready and only had a further five minutes if she was not to be late.

She gave her appearance a cursory glance. The dress was a strange shade of duck-egg blue with darker blue flowers embroidered around the neck and hem. She was grateful for the matching spencer as February was not the time to be parading around in a gown with short sleeves.

Her riding boots would look ridiculous with this ensemble and she could not squash her feet into the slippers offered to her. 'I shall have to go down in my stockings, I cannot dally any longer.'

There was no need for her to be escorted as she was well able to find her way. She hurried across the hallway, amused to find the smelly object she'd left had already been removed. This time a young footman was there to escort her to the breakfast parlour.

She stepped into the room with a minute to spare. The duke was waiting by the sideboard, a plate in his hand. 'In the nick of time, my dear. Now, I am famished and I imagine that you must be also. Allow me to serve you — is there anything in particular you would like?'

'I have an aversion to mushrooms but anything else would be wonderful. I hope that is coffee I can smell — that is my absolute passion.' She sat down at the centre table and eagerly poured herself a brimming cup of the aromatic brew she loved so much. She had scarcely taken a few appreciative sips when an overladen plate was placed in front of her.

'Good grief! I shall never eat all this, your grace. There's enough for a small army.' She viewed the three slices of crisp bacon, three eggs, fried potatoes and various slices of cold cuts with amusement. 'Nevertheless, I shall do my best as I hate to see good food wasted.'

Moments later he joined her at the table and his plate was even more laden than hers. He also helped himself to coffee, and for the next quarter of an hour neither spoke as they attempted to demolish their substantial breakfasts.

'I am defeated, I can eat no more. Indeed, I doubt I shall be able to eat again for a month.' She placed her cutlery on the plate and reached out for the coffee jug.

'Allow me to replenish your cup, my dear. Are you sure I cannot tempt you to pastries or more toast?' He filled her cup and sat back. 'I must say I admire a young lady with a healthy appetite. I cannot abide young women who pick at their food.'

'There's no danger of my doing that, your grace.' She gestured towards his empty plate. 'I believe that enjoying our food is something we have in common.'

His eyes flashed with something she didn't understand. 'I'm quite sure, my lady, that we are compatible in other ways.'

Unaccountably her cheeks flushed. Surely he was not flirting with her? 'The baby we rescued, your grace, comes from a good home. He is well-fed, happy, and was dressed in expensive garments. I am at a loss to understand how he came to be under the bushes in Green Park.'

He took her lead and the awkward moment passed. 'I also, on reflection, think the child was not there long. Although distressed, he was not cold or hungry. If he had been out all night I doubt he would have survived.'

'What are we to do with him? I have been thinking about this conundrum and have come to the conclusion he wasn't abducted in the normal fashion — which would be for the kidnappers to demand a ransom for his safe return. He was too easily found. Anyone on foot would have immediately seen him.'

'I agree with you.' He pushed his chair back and dropped his napkin on his plate. 'Come, shall we continue this conversation in my study?'

'Your study?' She wasn't sure this was the most appropriate place to be closeted alone with him.

'If you wish to be warm, then my study is the place to go. I only have fires in rooms that are in regular use.'

'Of course. My query was merely that in my household my father's study is sacrosanct and no females are allowed in there under any circumstances.'

'As there are no females in my household apart from my staff, I've not had to make a decision of that sort.'

He stood to one side to allow her to exit first and then strolled beside her the short distance to his domain. 'No doubt you have observed, being an intelligent young lady, that I reside down here. I cannot afford to keep the entire house warm, so just have fires in the staff quarters and the three rooms that I use.'

She was shocked by his frankness — surely discussing his lack of funds was not fitting? He ushered her into the study which had a large fire burning merrily in the grate. The furniture was worn, but comfortable, and the room, despite its dilapidation, had a welcoming feel. He pointed to a comfortable padded armchair and he folded his long length onto the Chesterfield placed opposite.

There was no time for her to dwell on his revelations as he wished to discuss the foundling. 'I have cancelled the visit of the physician as the child obviously is in perfect health. Two of my grooms have gone to search the area more thoroughly. They will also make enquiries in Piccadilly and the surrounding streets. It will be the servants who have the information we require.'

'I have been at a loss to come up with a sensible reason for this abandonment. I believe we are both of the opinion that the perpetrator meant for the infant to be found — so his demise was not part of the plan. Is this some sort of childish prank, do you think?'

'A jealous sibling? I cannot see that fits the bill. What would be gained?'

He tugged at his cravat, drawing her attention to the strong column of his neck. Her heart skipped a beat and she looked away to hide her interest.

'Lady Patience? A response would be

helpful, my dear.'

'I beg your pardon, your grace, I was wool-gathering. Let us consider the facts we know.' She counted on her fingers as she spoke. 'One — the baby is from a good home. Two — he wasn't left to perish. Three — ' She clapped her hands to her mouth as a possible solution occurred to her. 'I believe the baby was left for someone specific to find. Think about it, your grace, we were out earlier than anyone might expect. I think that my first suggestion was correct — this is indeed an abduction of some sort but we inadvertently prevented it.'

'Devil take it! You are right, my dear.' He sat upright on the sofa, his extraordinary dark eyes alight with excitement. 'A nursemaid must have taken the child to the park and then returned to the house. Her accomplice was no doubt somewhere in the vicinity when you arrived and ruined their plans.'

'Do you think so? I didn't see anyone — but then I wasn't looking. All we have to do is discover where the child was taken from and return him. It shouldn't be too difficult for his parents to discover which of their employees was involved.'

'Excellent! We should go out at once and make enquiries. I shall have my carriage brought round as soon as my men return and then we can begin our search.'

'I really should be getting back to Hanover Square, your grace. Lady Harriet and my cousin will be wondering what is keeping me here.'

'I told you, I sent a note round. Why should Aunt Harry object to you being in my company? After all, I am your temporary guardian, am I not?'

She had no ready answer for this. She was beginning to feel events were moving out of her control, that circumstances were conspiring to put her in an impossible situation. The longer she spent in his company the more difficult it was going to be to reveal the truth.

He stood up. 'Remain here, I shall

see if I have the news we are waiting for. I'll get my housekeeper to find you a warm cloak and bonnet.' He grinned and nodded to her stockinged feet which she had inadvertently allowed to peep from beneath her skirt. 'Perhaps you had better put your boots on; they will not look so outlandish when you have on outdoor garments.'

He strode off leaving her confused. He was overfond of issuing instructions, but then she supposed a duke must expect his orders to be obeyed. However, she had no intention of remaining in the study, she would go and find a suitable cloak and bonnet and put on her boots.

As she was approaching the grand entrance hall she heard voices. She increased her pace and arrived in a rush to discover her cousin and Lady Harriet entering through the front door.

5

'Lady Harriet, I'm so glad to see you. I have had such an adventure this morning; you will not believe it when I tell you.'

'You are wearing no footwear, Lady Patience, might I enquire as to why that is?'

'I'm just going to put my boots back on, my lady, then I shall be ready to leave. I sincerely hope that the groom has returned Trojan to your stables in my absence.' She wasn't sure if she should direct Lady Harriet to the study or leave her standing where she was.

'Run along, I shall wait here until you both return. No doubt my nephew will return momentarily and explain exactly what is going on.'

Charity grabbed her cousin's hand and half-dragged her up the stairs and back to the icy bedchamber in which she had changed earlier. As soon as they were private she blurted out the events of the morning.

'How lucky you are to have had such an adventure — I wish now I had agreed to come with you. I had to persuade Lady Harriet to come and collect you as she was determined to leave you here for as long as possible.'

'I must just put on my boots and find a cloak and bonnet and then I am ready to return. I have a horrible feeling that you are the intended bride for the duke. He was quite open in admitting he has debts. I'm sure that is why Lady Harriet was happy to leave me here despite the irregularity of the situation.'

Instead of being horrified Patience giggled. 'In which case, they will both be sadly disappointed when they discover our deception. Thank God we decided to change places, I have no wish to be put in the invidious position of having to turn down such an eligible bachelor.'

The boots were where she'd left them

and she soon found a thick woollen cloak to cover her flimsy gown. 'There are no bonnets here that I can borrow, I shall just have to hope no one notices my lack of decorum.' She smiled as she recalled she had already scandalised the duke by removing her skirt in public. 'It would not be fair to lead him on, Patience, he is a kind man and does not deserve to be deceived.'

'Fiddlesticks to that! It is he who is perpetrating a deception, my love. We were only invited here so that he could see if I would suit. I should have realised there was an ulterior motive in my godmother's unexpected invitation. They will be hoist by their own petard and I for one think it will serve them right.'

Patience shook her head and then stepped across to embrace her. 'Please, do not look so woebegone. Once word gets out that he is looking for a bride there will be a queue of hopeful heiresses flocking to his feet. He will be spoilt for choice and will no doubt find someone more to his liking than you.'

Charity wasn't sure how she felt about this comment so refrained from replying. 'I am ready and I wish to leave before the duke returns. Although you seem unbothered by continuing this charade I am uncomfortable with it and intend to spend as little time in his company as I can. In fact, I believe I shall contract some highly contagious illness and be obliged to remain in my apartment for the foreseeable future.'

Her ridiculous statement lightened the atmosphere and they were both laughing as they ran downstairs. There was no sign of Lady Harriet, but the front door was ajar and they dashed through to see the carriage waiting outside.

Charity scrambled in, unsurprised to find it empty. 'Lady Harriet must be with the duke, had we better return to the house and wait for her there?'

'No, I've just instructed the coach-man to take us home and then return for her immediately. The horses have been standing around quite long enough; she will understand why we have gone on without her.'

As the vehicle rocked away Charity viewed her cousin with disquiet. 'What are you up to, Patience? I have no wish to be embroiled in any further escapades in your name, I do assure you.'

'I wish to visit the menagerie and, as soon as you have changed into something more suitable, we shall go there. We will take our maids and two footmen so there will be no objection on that score.'

Relieved it was no more than that, she sank back on the squabs. 'We shall have to wait until your godmother returns with the carriage; we can hardly walk all the way to the menagerie.'

'You are forgetting, my love, that my own carriage is still in London. We shall take that and thus inconvenience nobody by our absence.'

★   ★   ★

When they returned from their excursion it was late afternoon and the streets were full of ladies in carriages returning from their morning calls. Charity thought calling these visits 'morning calls' quite ridiculous as they never took place until after midday. Mama had explained to her that ladies never rose before noon so therefore everyone considered morning to stretch from breakfast until dinner. This meant that afternoon did not exist in London.

Once safely in their apartment Charity felt it safe to speak freely. 'I enjoyed the visit, thank you for arranging it, Patience. I suppose we shall have to go down for dinner tonight, we can hardly lurk in our chamber a second time.'

'I am looking forward to it. Don't you want to wear one of my evening gowns and pretend to be a lady?'

'I do not. The sooner this nonsense is over the happier I shall be. By the way, why did your maid wander off during our visit?'

'She had an errand to run for me,

nothing of importance I do assure you.' She yawned loudly. 'I intend to take a nap, are you not going to do the same? You must be exhausted after all the excitement of today. I wonder if the duke has discovered the baby's parents yet.'

'I intend to go downstairs and speak to Lady Harriet on that very subject. I am not at all fatigued, but you must rest if you feel tired. I shall return in an hour to change for dinner.'

The footman allocated to them jumped to attention as she appeared. 'Thank you, but we no longer require your services as we are now well able to find the way for ourselves around this vast establishment.' He bowed and vanished through a door she had not noticed in the panelling.

The double doors to the drawing room were open and Charity sailed in without stopping to think that the room might be occupied by more than her hostess. Three smartly dressed matrons, accompanied by their equally elegant daughters, turned to look at her.

She curtsied and was relieved she had put on one of the more fetching gowns that her cousin had given her. 'I beg your pardon, Lady Harriet, I did not mean to intrude.'

'Come in, Patience, my dear, let me make you known to my friends.'

By the time the introductions were complete Charity had forgotten all the names. She curtsied and simpered and replied when spoken to and felt like a fish out of water. She was relieved when the tea was drunk, gloves were put on by the visitors and reticules collected.

They were families with excellent pedigrees, all with titles of some sort, and she was fairly sure that one of the girls had taken her in dislike. No doubt this antipathy was caused because the young lady in question had set her sights on the duke and saw her as a rival.

She slipped away to her apartment whilst the farewells were being said for she had no longer wished for a private conversation with Lady Harriet. The covert looks and insincere smiles directed at her just served to confirm her fears — she (or rather her cousin) had been selected to be the next bride for the duke. Now she had been introduced to Lady Harriet's cronies as her cousin, it would no longer be so easy to extricate herself from this dilemma.

There was a little over an hour before dinner would be served, more than enough time to get ready as she had no intention of having her hair arranged in an elaborate style and she had no jewellery to wear.

Her cousin was awake and already about her toilette. The maid, another Mary, designated to take care of her pounced on her eagerly. 'My lady, Miss Lawson suggested I put out all your gowns so you can select which one you wish to wear.'

The array of shimmering silk draped across the end of the bed made her spoilt for choice. 'What are you wearing, dearest? I do not wish to choose something that will clash with your ensemble.'

'I am wearing the pink gown with the *demi-train* — it's the one on the rail over there.'

'In which case, I shall take the pale green with the spangled overskirt.'

There was no opportunity to talk whilst their abigails were in attendance but as soon as they had been dismissed Charity voiced her concerns. 'I cannot continue with this charade, Patience, the longer it goes on the more difficult it will be to explain why we did it.'

'Papa does not wish me to marry until I reach my majority so we are merely following his instructions by removing me from the marriage mart. We are so alike that I doubt anyone, apart from those most closely involved, will be any the wiser when we do reveal our true identities.'

'I had no opportunity to ask Lady Harriet if the duke had discovered the whereabouts of the baby's parents. I shall do so immediately. No doubt she will wish to know our plans for tomorrow and I was rather hoping you would join me for an early morning ride. I have no wish to go out alone again with the duke. My appearing at his side will merely add fuel to the fire of speculation.'

On the way downstairs they complimented each other on their appearance. Tonight her cousin had restrained her curls and, dressed as they were in similar gowns, they could easily be mistaken for identical twins.

The usual two footmen were waiting to announce them which she thought a trifle ostentatious for a quiet family dinner. However as she walked into the drawing room she was shocked to see the duke, magnificent in evening black, standing with his back to the fire watching their approach.

He bowed. 'Good evening, Lady Patience, Miss Lawson.' He stared at Charity and then at her cousin and shook his head. 'Dressed as you are you are almost indistinguishable.' He smiled directly at her. 'I have news for you, Lady Patience, I am sure you wish to know what transpired after you left so abruptly this morning.'

'Indeed I do, your grace, I have thought of little else all day.' Belatedly she remembered her manners and curtsied to Lady Harriet who nodded regally from her position by the fire.

'Come in, girls, we have a little while before dinner is served. Would you care to join me in a glass of sweet sherry wine?'

'I thank you, but no.' Charity turned to the duke who had been watching this exchange with interest. 'Tell me, your grace, did you find the infant's abode? Were things as you suspected?'

'Unfortunately, the baby remains in my care as my enquiries in the vicinity were unable to locate the household from which he had been stolen. My housekeeper has named him Richard and the little chap seems quite happy with her choice.'

'If he is a child of a wealthy family as

we suspect, then surely his disappearance will be a topic of conversation all over Town.'

'One would think so, but I have visited my clubs and heard nothing on the subject there.' He turned to Lady Harriet. 'I believe you mentioned the baby during your at-home this afternoon, Aunt Harry. Did you get any information from your friends?'

'None at all, they were shocked, but could offer no suggestions as to where the child came from. Lady Frances is an inveterate gossip, I am certain she will spread the news and recover any titbits pertinent to the subject and return them to me.'

When the butler announced that dinner was served they all moved towards the door. Although Lady Harriet insisted the meal was informal, there were several removes and three courses. The conversation was entertaining but Charity was relieved when it was over and she could retire to the drawing room leaving the duke to drink port.

Lady Harriet introduced the subject of their plans. 'Well, girls, are you intending to visit more sights tomorrow? I would like to take you on my morning calls, so you must ensure you are here by two o'clock.'

'We intend to ride, Lady Harriet, and then visit Hatchards. However, we will be home long before two o'clock.'

If Lady Harriet thought it strange Miss Lawson had replied and not her goddaughter, she made no comment. Charity decided she had better participate in the conversation. 'When do we make our appearance in public, Lady Harriet? Obviously not until our new wardrobe arrives, but we would both like to know what invitations you have received on our behalf.'

'I thought a musicale would be ideal for your first venture into society, my dear. You both have sufficient gowns to attend something so informal. Although provincially made, I defy any lady to detect that your outfits are anything but the first stare of fashion.'

Her cousin joined in. 'When is this event, Lady Harriet? I have never attended anything so exciting and cannot thank you enough for including me in your kind invitation.'

This was doing it rather too brown and Charity gave her cousin a warning pinch. Lady Harriet smiled and nodded, the ruby in her turban sparkling in the firelight.

'The event is in two days' time, Miss Lawson, and will be held at the home of Sir James and Lady Bridges. You met her this afternoon, my dear.'

'Yes, of course I did. Her daughter was the young lady with dark hair and pretty green eyes.'

'Miss Imogen Bridges is expected to make a hit this Season. Although there are some that say her fortune comes from trade as it was her maternal grand-father who left her a vast fortune. He made his money in manufacturing of some sort.'

'I liked her, I hope she finds someone to her liking and is not pushed into a business arrangement.' No sooner had she spoken than Charity regretted her words, especially as the duke strolled in and must have overheard.

'Lady Bridges is determined her daughter will marry well and I'm sure the girl will do what is expected of her.'

Patience wriggled beside her and Charity knew her cousin was going to say something outrageous. She was not disappointed.

'Forgive me for saying so, my lady, but there must be several aristocratic gentlemen in need of an heiress to restore their fortunes. Miss Bridges should have no difficulty finding a husband with a suitable title.' She smiled sweetly at the duke and his eyes narrowed.

Charity could see he wasn't amused and rather thought him a dangerous man to annoy. 'Your grace, is there anything you would like me to do to help find the baby's parents?'

'No, thank you. However, if you wish to come and see Richard at any time you would be most welcome in the nursery.'

This would not be a good idea in the circumstances, although she really would like to spend time with the infant she had been instrumental in rescuing — possibly from a horrible fate. 'Perhaps my cousin and I could call in tomorrow morning? We will be riding in Green Park, and St James's Square is no distance from there.'

He frowned. 'I cannot permit you to ride about Town without a suitable escort. What time do you wish me to call for you both?'

'We intend to take two grooms, that could hardly be considered unescorted.'

'I apologise for being abrupt, my dear, I keep forgetting that you are a country miss and not aware of the etiquette of Town.'

Charity bridled at his casual comment. Not only did he consider her ignorant, but also obliged to follow his autocratic instructions. He might consider himself to have authority over her, but she did not. She kept her expression bland as she replied. 'We shall be leaving at nine o'clock, I hope that is convenient for you.'

He was equally urbane as he answered. 'I'm looking forward to it, my dear, having two delightful young ladies at my side will raise my status no end.'

Her cousin missed the irony of his statement. 'I cannot believe being seen with us will improve your condition one jot. No doubt if you should just raise one finger you would be swamped by eager young ladies wishing to accompany you to Green Park.'

He laughed at her nonsense and Charity found herself warming to him, despite the fact that his intentions were to entice the girl he thought to be an heiress and an aristocrat into accepting his offer.

'I fear that you are right, Miss Lawson, it's for that very reason I would rather have my teeth pulled than go to Almack's. However, I shall do my duty by the pair of you and escort you to whatever overcrowded, unpleasant, boring event you might wish to attend.'

'Good heavens, your grace, we are overwhelmed by your enthusiasm and must thank you profusely. I cannot tell you how much I'm looking forward to being escorted to my first ball by an elderly, curmudgeonly gentleman.' Charity rounded her eyes and attempted to hold back a laugh.

Lady Harriet exclaimed in shock at her description of her handsome nephew, who could not be a day older than one and thirty. Patience collapsed in a fit of giggles and was forced to hide her face in her reticule.

His rich, dark chuckle sent shivers of an unexpected kind down her spine and his eyes glinted with a darkness she didn't recognise. Embarrassed by her reaction, she jumped up, mumbled an apology, and ran away before her discomfiture was revealed.

6

Hugo barely had time to scramble to his feet before the girl left the room. Her cousin immediately stood up and curtsied. 'I beg your pardon, Lady Harriet, your grace, I shall also retire.' With a swirl of silk she too vanished.

'How extraordinary! The young people of today have no respect for the older generation. I am beginning to regret inviting those girls to stay — the Season is not started and already they are giving me palpitations.'

'I hardly think that rescuing an infant in the park can be put down to bad manners, Aunt Harry,' he said with a smile. 'However, our ruse has been discovered. Both girls are well aware of my interest in your goddaughter and if tonight's performance is anything to go by, neither of them is impressed by my credentials.'

'Fustian! The chit will do as she is told. You are the catch of the Season and her parents will be overjoyed when you make the girl an offer.'

He had remained on his feet and decided to take his leave. Fond as he was of his aunt, he had seen rather too much of her these past few days. 'I bid you good night, Aunt Harry, no doubt I will see you tomorrow evening at the musicale. As you are accompanying your charges it won't be necessary for me to come here to collect them. I hardly think they need my august presence beside them for something so innocuous.'

'Good night, my boy, and thank you for your interest. I do hope you soon find the owners of that baby — yours is a bachelor establishment and not best suited to the care of an infant.'

He collected his topcoat, hat and cane and left. The night was young; he would stroll to his club and play a game or two of cards before he returned home.

He enjoyed walking about the streets

unaccompanied. Although a possible target for footpads and vagrants he rarely left the more frequented streets so was not unduly bothered he would be accosted. He carried his cane not for affectation, but for protection.

As he walked he considered his options. He had no wish to marry a girl who didn't want him, and from the way his quarry had behaved he was certain she did not view his interest with favour.

It was a damned nuisance Miss Lawson had revealed his true intentions. Maybe he should move on and search for a more willing partner, but there was something about Patience that intrigued him.

He didn't believe there was another young lady in the city who would have done as she had. She was as kind as she was beautiful. He halted in mid-stride. God's teeth! Had he fallen under her spell so quickly? He was looking for a match with a young lady who would not drive him to drink with her vacuous comments, and was sufficiently comely to make sharing the marriage bed a pleasure rather than a chore.

Love did not enter into the equation. Respect and compatibility were far more important in his opinion. In fact, love was a messy emotion which made sensible gentlemen behave like idiots. His mouth twitched at the nonsensical notion of being driven to write poetry to a young lady to express one's undying devotion.

No — it would be far safer to remove himself from temptation and look elsewhere for his bride. In future he would keep his distance, only visit when he had to and under no circumstances ask the young lady to stand up with him. He would send word that he could not accompany the girls on their ride as he had an urgent business meeting.

* * *

The next morning Charity was dressed in her own habit, a plain blue ensemble, with no decoration apart from a set of handsome silver buttons, and ready to ride, but her cousin was still in bed. 'Patience, I thought you were coming with me. If we want to be away from here before the duke arrives we must leave immediately.'

'I have changed my mind, you must go on your own. I have a headache and shall remain in bed until it is time to get ready to go out with Lady Harriet.'

'You are perfectly well, cousin, so don't prevaricate. I cannot go out without you, so get up at once if you please.'

'I will come but only if you promise to accompany me when we get back.' Her cousin sprung out of bed and was in her habit in minutes. She wore a cherry-red worsted that was as bright as the ruined blue outfit but fortunately without extra embellishment.

'We have already planned on visiting the bookshop on our return. Do you have another excursion in mind?'

'I had forgotten we were going to Hatchards, but that will do very well.'

Charity wasn't sure what this cryptic comment meant, but had no time to discuss it further as her cousin rushed from the room leaving her no option but to follow.

Trojan was saddled and waiting for her and a pretty grey mare had been chosen for her cousin. Two grooms were to accompany them today and she hoped this would be sufficient to keep their reputations intact.

As they were about to leave she turned to the head groom. 'It is possible the duke will arrive expecting to ride with us. If he does, will you offer our apologies?'

The excursion was most enjoyable and they returned to find the stable yard quiet. They dismounted and handed the reins to the grooms who had accompanied them. There was no sign of the duke and Charity was relieved there would be no confrontation over their rudeness.

They had yet to breakfast so decided to send for a tray and eat whilst they got ready to go out again. Her cousin spent an age selecting her outfit. She held up yet another gown, this one in a similar cherry red and a bonnet that looked remarkably like a coal scuttle.

'What about this? I do wish to look my best on my first real excursion.'

'I like it as much as I did all the others — in fact as it has far fewer bows and rouleau, I think it will do very well. I heard our breakfast arriving next door, and the chocolate will be undrinkable if we delay much longer.'

Mary and Sally were to accompany them as well as two footmen to carry any purchases they might make. 'We should be able to walk to Piccadilly and be back in plenty of time to change for our morning calls.' Charity wished she had worn something a little more dramatic as this morning they looked more like their normal personas. Her borrowed gown was gold with pink embroidery and a matching pelisse of pink. The bonnet, although somewhat less ostentatious than her cousin's, was still over-adorned with artificial fruit.

She had discovered the duke had cried off this morning's ride — was he too having second thoughts about his deception?

There had been no sign of Lady Harriet — no doubt she, like other ladies of fashion, remained in her boudoir until midday. The weather was surprisingly clement for the end of February and the pavements were bustling with like-minded ladies.

'Have you noticed, Patience, that not every young lady is accompanied by a bevy of servants? Perhaps next time we can come out with just Mary and Sally and leave the footmen behind.'

The bookshop was everything she'd hoped and she was soon lost amongst the shelves. Sally had remained with her but her cousin and Mary were no longer in sight. The store was full of other well-to-do folk but despite wearing a cherry-red bucket on her head, and being taller than most young women, her cousin was not visible amongst the milling throng.

'Sally, I cannot see Miss Lawson. We must search thoroughly together. I shall go this way and you go the other and we will meet at the door.'

After twenty minutes Charity admitted defeat. Her cousin had left Hatchards. There was only one reason she could think of and that was because Patience had a clandestine assignation with Mr Pettigrew. Her heart sank to her boots. This visit to London, her inclusion, the switching of places, all had been done with deliberation in order to allow for this secret meeting.

If they should be discovered her cousin's good name would be gone and nobody, not even an impecunious duke, would offer for her. This mysterious Mr Pettigrew knew her cousin's true identity and was no doubt planning to compromise her so she would be obliged to marry him.

She was at a loss to know what to do.

She could hardly go in search of her cousin — that would just be adding fuel to the fire. And anyway, she had no idea in which direction Patience had gone. She stepped out onto the path and looked anxiously in both directions but did not see her cousin. However, the very last person she wished to meet at that very moment was striding towards her.

'Lady Patience, I must apologise for not keeping my appointment with you this morning.' Hugo quirked an eyebrow. 'I assume that you went out as planned and quite ignored my instructions.'

She hid her blushes in her bonnet brim. 'I must admit that we did, your grace, but I can assure you that we saw several other young ladies riding with only a groom beside them so I'm quite sure we were not breaking any rules.'

He looked over her shoulder and then his expression changed. 'Where is your companion? I take it you're not here alone?'

'No, sir, I am just waiting for my

cousin to complete her purchases and then we shall go home directly. Do not let me keep you from your business, I am sure you are on your way to an important business engagement. You could not possibly have come here deliberately to meet with us.' She smiled sweetly and saw she had made a direct hit.

He ran his finger around his neck-cloth as if it had unaccountably grown tighter. 'You have found me out, my dear, I felt badly about not appearing this morning so have come here instead to escort you home.' He glanced at Sally who was conspicuously without a brown paper parcel in her hands. 'Have you not bought yourself any books? Surely that was the object of the exercise?'

She was falling deeper and deeper into a tangle of her own deceit. She would not tell further lies, she would explain why she was dithering in the street. 'Miss Lawson and her maid have disappeared, your grace, I fear she has a secret assignation with a gentleman called Mr Pettigrew. Her parents are unaware of this acquaintance and would be horrified if they knew.' She almost told him the whole, revealed who she was, but something held her back.

'Devil take it! If the man's so unsuitable he would not do for a vicar's daughter, then he must be a villain indeed. I can see no reason otherwise why Pettigrew did not call on your uncle and make his intentions known.'

She must own up; until he knew that her cousin was the heiress he would not take the situation seriously. 'Your grace — '

'Go home, say nothing to Lady Harriet, make sure your girl is discreet. I will find Miss Lawson and return her to you.' He gave her no time to answer before continuing. 'I need to know what she is wearing — I don't suppose you have any idea what this Pettigrew fellow looks like?'

'I have never met him and she didn't

describe him to me. My cousin is wearing a cherry-red ensemble with an extraordinary bonnet. There cannot be any other young lady quite so distinctively dressed.'

'Excellent — that'll make it so much easier. Before you go, there is something I wish to say to you. After your cousin's scandalous behaviour you must have her return home at once before she can damage your reputation.'

'I shall do no such thing, and I thank you not to interfere. There will be a perfectly reasonable explanation. I imagine they must be in love and wish to snatch a few secret moments together.' She glared at him and he returned the look in good measure.

'I will not discuss the matter in the middle of the street, young lady, but be very sure there will be a reckoning for both of you. I take my duties as your temporary guardian seriously and have the written permission of both your parents, and your cousin's, to take whatever action I consider appropriate if you misbehave.'

She was tempted to kick him hard on the shins for his high-handed statement. However, she would restrain herself until he found Patience and restored her safely to Hanover Square. She ignored his remark, rudely turned her back and marched away with her head in the air.

★ ★ ★

Hugo watched her go and despite his annoyance he could not help but admire her bravery. There were few of his acquaintance who would dare to gainsay him. Her abigail was obliged to run in order to keep up with her mistress. He had come particularly to tell Patience some interesting information he had gleaned about Richard. This would have to wait until he had recovered the tiresome Miss Lawson.

He stood for a moment allowing pedestrians to flow around him whilst he considered the situation. Where would Pettigrew take a young lady for a few stolen minutes? He came to the conclusion that the safest thing would be to hide in plain sight. If he were in the same position he would stroll quite openly up and down Piccadilly as if he and the young lady were affianced. As Miss Lawson had her maid with her, and was unknown in London, she should come out of this unscathed.

He stepped to the edge of the pavement so that from his superior height he could view the street in both directions. Good grief! Patience had not been jesting when she had described her cousin's bonnet as extraordinary. Both ladies and gentlemen were stopping to gawp at Miss Lawson as she walked arm in arm with the young man who must be the mysterious Pettigrew.

The gentleman was attracting as much attention as his companion, as he was wearing the most outlandish waistcoat with purple and green stripes and his collar was so high he could look neither left nor right. There was nothing startling about Pettigrew, apart from his garments — he was of medium height, stocky build and nondescript brown hair.

Hugo schooled his features; he had no intention of creating a scene in public. However, he would leave the young man in no doubt that he intended to pursue the matter to the gentleman's detriment. He stepped into the shadows and waited patiently for the errant couple to reach him. He stepped out and nodded politely.

'Miss Lawson, I have been waiting here to escort you home.' He fixed the young man with an arctic stare. 'Pettigrew, I expect to see you at my house in St James's Square at three o'clock this afternoon. Do not be late.' He allowed Pettigrew no time to respond and took Miss Lawson's limp hand and placed it on his arm. He was relieved to see her maid had remained at her side throughout this disgraceful episode.

He felt the hesitation in her step. He paused and spoke softly to her. 'You will not make a scene, you will walk quietly beside me and pretend that you are happy to do so. Do I make myself clear?'

The girl gulped, nodded and bowed her head making it impossible to see her face. They walked for half a mile before she spoke. 'Your grace, I beg you do not tell my parents, they would not understand. I have fallen in love with Mr Pettigrew and he with me — but we cannot marry until I reach my majority in two years' time.'

He didn't answer immediately; he needed to think about his response. She sounded sincere and this changed his view of the episode. The young man, apart from his ridiculous clothes, had seemed a harmless enough sort of fellow, not at all what he'd been expecting. Pettigrew was hardly the wicked seducer he had anticipated.

'I had intended to send you home in disgrace, young lady, with a letter for your parents. However, I shall reserve my decision until I have spoken to Pettigrew this afternoon. You will remain in the house and not attend any social functions until I give you leave to do so. Do you understand?'

'I do, your grace.'

She offered no apology for inconveniencing him or upsetting her cousin and this omission gave him pause for thought. Surely if she was truly repentant, and understood how disgraceful her behaviour had been, she would be eager to apologise? He stared thoughtfully at the top of her ridiculous bonnet. There was more to this than a clandestine walk — the chit was up to something and he was determined to discover what this was.

Less than a week ago he was leading a quiet, uneventful existence with nothing more exciting to consider than how he was to pay the next quarter's bills, and here he was up to his neck in intrigues and abductions. He had never felt so well in his life.

He released his grip on Miss Lawson's arm when they reached the front steps of Aunt Harry's house. She shot off like a scalded rabbit leaving him to enter on his own. The first person he saw was Patience, still in her outdoor garments, staring in bewilderment as her cousin vanished up the stairs.

7

Charity turned to face the duke who was watching her intently from across the vestibule. 'Thank you for returning my cousin, sir, you have arrived so promptly I am assuming that nothing untoward had time to take place. What of Mr Pettigrew?'

'Are we to stand and converse out here, my dear? I would much prefer to continue our conversation in the drawing room.'

The last thing she wanted was a private conversation with this gentleman. The more she saw of him the less she trusted her volatile emotions. She could not allow herself to become attached to him in any way. He had been quite open about his need to marry an heiress of impeccable breeding and she failed on both counts. A vicar's daughter with a negligible dowry would be a totally unsuitable bride for a duke.

She dropped in a curtsy. 'I apologise, your grace, but I must go to my cousin immediately. No doubt she will tell me the whole. Thank you for your intervention, it is most appreciated.' She turned and was about to flee up the stairs when by some extraordinary happenstance he was blocking her path. How could such a big man move so fast?

'Miss Lawson will do very well without you, my dear, however, I will not. I must insist that you accompany me to the drawing room.' If he had accompanied this command with an autocratic look she would have refused, but he smiled at her in that particular way of his and she could not.

'Very well, it would seem that I have no recourse but to do as you say.' Then for no reason at all she laughed. 'To be honest, sir, I would much rather have your unbiased opinion of what happened than listen to my cousin's fabrications. Also, I am agog to know if you are any nearer to finding Richard's parents.'

She was about to go with him to the drawing room when he restrained her with a gentle hand on her arm. 'Are you not going to remove your coat and bonnet, my dear? I hardly think you will need them inside.'

What was she thinking of? He made her flustered and behave like a ninny-hammer. She could hardly remove her pelisse and bonnet in front of him — there had been enough scandalous behaviour from her cousin for one morning.

'How silly! I shall not be above a few moments, your grace, perhaps you would care to order refreshments whilst you wait?'

He chuckled and shook his head. 'I have your measure, sweetheart, I have no intention of letting you out of my sight.' Before she could prevent him he deftly untied the bow under her chin and removed her bonnet. She was so taken aback by his strange behaviour she remained rooted to the spot when, if she'd had any sense, she would have run away.

'There, that is so much better. Now, can you manage the buttons or shall I assist you further?'

With fumbling fingers she hastily undid her coat and slipped it off — but was then at a loss to know what to do with it. He was still holding her bonnet and some impulse made her drape her pelisse over his arm as if he were a coat stand. Then she skipped away leaving him to deal with both her outer garments and his own when there was no sign of a footman or parlourmaid to take them from him.

He was right behind her as she entered the drawing room and still carrying his burden. To her astonishment he tossed her things on a chair and his own quickly followed. She looked around for a bell-strap so she could summon an elusive footman and order coffee and pastries for them both. She spied what she wanted to the right of the cheerily burning logs. Without stopping to think she rushed across, sending her skirts swirling into the flames.

Before she could react he was beside her, threw her to the floor and rolled her in the rug. He then proceeded to bang her lower regions with more vigour than was called for. She was unable to move, only her head protruded, her limbs were trapped inside and he seemed in no hurry to release her.

She recovered her breath and spat out the grit from her mouth. 'Stop your pummelling, I am no longer in any danger. Kindly remove yourself so that I may get free.'

He sat back on his knees but kept one hand firmly on the end of the carpet so she could not get out. 'What in God's name were you thinking of? Do you have feathers between your ears? You could have been badly burnt.'

At least he had stopped slapping her, which was a start. 'Am I to be allowed to get up, your grace, or am I to remain here like a pig in a blanket indefinitely?'

He stared at her as if she were speaking a foreign tongue and then his expression changed. 'What am I thinking of? I beg your pardon, allow me to assist you to your feet.' Without further ado he put his arms around her and the carpet and stood up as if she weighed nothing at all. Then he proceeded to unroll her until she was free.

Something was sticking to her legs and she glanced down. She could not prevent a gasp escaping. The lower portion of her promenade dress was no more than a charred ruin. Even her petticoats were singed. Her knees buckled as the full impact of what had almost happened finally registered.

For the second time his arms were around her and he carried her to the nearest daybed and placed her on it. 'Lie still, sweetheart, let me look at your legs. I shall never forgive myself if because of my poor reactions you have been burned.'

If she hadn't felt so faint she would

have protested, demanded that he send for Sally, but her eyes were blurred and a horrible blackness threatened to overwhelm her. She closed her eyes and tried to ignore his gentle touch on her lower limbs as he checked for burns.

'No damage, apart from to your gown and underpinnings. You can open your eyes now, my dear, your ordeal is over.'

She risked a peep and found him sitting, far too close, on the same *chaise longue* as her. He shouldn't be there — what if anyone came in and found him in such a compromising position? She pushed herself upright and attempted to swing her legs to the floor but he prevented this by remaining where he was.

'I wish to go upstairs at once and change my gown, your grace. I cannot possibly remain in here with you in such disarray.'

He smiled and shook his head. 'You are going nowhere unless you're pre-pared to let me carry you. You have undergone a severe shock to the system, I doubt you would reach your apartment without having a fit of the vapours.'

She recoiled at the very idea of being transported like a parcel about the place in full view of any member of staff who cared to watch. 'I shall stay where I am until I feel more the thing. Could I prevail upon you, sir, to ring for coffee and pastries? I was about to do so before I went up in flames.'

His snort of laughter was contagious and she giggled. 'I shall do so at once, I'm sure we could both do with some sustenance after the dramas of this morning.' He didn't pull the bell-strap but strode to the doors and shouted for attention.

His outrageous behaviour made her laugh again and at the sound he glanced over his shoulder and winked.

A footman almost fell over himself in his eagerness to respond and was sent at a run to the kitchen to fulfil their order. He collected a chair and seated himself within arm's reach of her. Far too close for her equanimity.

They chatted of this and that whilst they waited for the food to arrive — her head was spinning and she wasn't entirely sure if this was due to his proximity or was the result of her brush with conflagration. She had the distinct impression he was flirting with her, enjoying her discomfiture and deliberately larding his conversation with unwanted and inappropriate endearments.

Two footmen galloped in with what looked like card tables. A parlourmaid whisked a white damask cloth over each like a magician and then two further minions staggered in with their food. The trays were placed on the waiting tables and then the duke waved everyone away. 'We shall serve ourselves, if we require anything else I shall shout for it.' He kept a commendably straight face as he said this but she was obliged to use her hand to hide her giggles.

Without a thought to the proprieties he closed the double doors on the faces of the startled servants. Then he waved at the laden tables. 'I suggest, sweetheart, that we help ourselves. There is such a miscellany of items upon these trays that it would take me as long to list them as for you to serve yourself.'

She smiled and indicated her ruined gown which he had carefully arranged so her stockings were not immodestly displayed. 'Not only am I too frail to fetch my own refreshments, your grace, but as you so kindly pointed out, I'm so feeble that I'm likely to succumb to a fit of the vapours if I should dare to stand up.'

He grinned and his eyes crinkled endearingly at the corners making him look years younger, boyish almost. 'How true, my angel. I hope my selection will meet with your approval.' Without asking her what she would like he heaped a random selection of items on a plate, grabbed the necessary cutlery and folded napkin and handed her everything at once.

She managed to take the plate without spilling anything but dropped the knife, fork and napkin. He sighed theatrically and retrieved them from the floor. With a solemn face he shook out the linen square and draped it over her lap. His hands didn't touch her, but he came so close she was able to inhale his distinctive aroma of what she thought might be lemon and saddle soap.

Flustered, she almost tipped her food into her lap. He wandered back to the table and filled his own plate, giving her time to recover her equilibrium. 'Coffee? No, I think it might be wise to give you that after you have finished your meal in case you spill it everywhere. I had not thought you a clumsy girl, but now I am reconsidering my opinion.'

He was being intentionally annoying and she responded in kind. She was holding the fork in her left hand and threw it with deadly accuracy at his derriere. The result was everything she'd hoped for as he leapt into the air sending the contents of his half-full plate in all directions. However, his language was something she hoped never to have the misfortune to hear again.

'I do beg your pardon, your grace, my hand slipped and my fork travelled of its own volition. I do hope you have not received a serious injury — ' She had been about to mention his posterior but restrained herself in time.

He put his plate down with deliberation. He stood with his back to her, gripping the edge of the table for a few seconds, and her stomach somersaulted. He was shaking with rage. She should not have done it. He slowly faced her and she held her breath.

She couldn't read his expression — didn't think he was enraged — but there was something she didn't quite like about his demeanour. Was he going to throw something in retaliation? He shook his head and folded his arms. 'I am at a loss for words, my dear, and that is not something I can recall happening to me before. I compliment you on the accuracy of your throw but warn you will have your comeuppance, maybe not today, maybe not tomorrow, but I promise you that when you are least expecting it I shall return the favour.'

He spun round and refilled his plate as if nothing untoward had happened. What the servants would think of the scattered food she had no idea, hopefully they would consider it merely a careless accident. There was also the discarded rug to think about — this had been flung into a corner and forgotten. She hoped that being a duke would mean such eccentric behaviour would be overlooked.

Dare she ask for coffee? She was parched and the tantalising smell from the silver coffee pot was too much to bear.

'Your grace, could I trouble you for some coffee before you sit down to eat? I am perfectly capable of managing both food and drink simultaneously.'

'Allow me to finish selecting my food

and then I shall attend to your request.'
He removed one of the trays and placed
it with the other, thus leaving an empty
table upon which he could put his
plate. With casual nonchalance he
fetched an upright chair, placed a
napkin and a knife and fork by his meal
and then moved across to pour them
both a drink. 'Cream and sugar? Or do
you prefer it black, as I do?'

She was mesmerised by his performance. Today he was wearing a superfine
jacket of dark blue, cut high at the front,
and so closely fitting she could see every
muscle in his back flexing as he moved.
Somehow he seemed a different man to
the one she'd seen three short days ago.
Even his clothes were changed — his
boots appeared to have a higher shine
than before and his stock seemed more
intricately tied.

He fetched her coffee and passed it to
her with a bow, but said nothing, then
strolled back to the table and began his
meal, ignoring her completely. She wasn't
sure if she was offended or relieved by

his behaviour. The appetising smell of warm game pie, fruit chutney and freshly baked bread overcame her irritation and she reached down to pick up her cutlery. Botheration! He had not returned her fork and she could hardly eat her meal with her fingers and a knife alone.

He was studiously ignoring her and tucking in with great relish. Her stomach rumbled at the thought of what she was missing. She had two choices: she could try and eat with a knife alone or walk across the room and reveal her legs in a most unseemly way.

Hunger won over decorum and she carefully placed her food, drink and napkin on the *chaise longue* and stood up. He was eating with such concentration she was sure she could recover her fork from the boards. She crept stealthily towards the item glinting on the floor and was about to recover it when he spun round.

She was so startled she fell backwards in an ignominious heap and exposed a shocking amount of lower limb to his interested gaze.

'Allow me, my dear, how remiss of me not to have returned the missile which you so kindly threw at me.' She was pink from her toes to her crown and unable to say a word in her defence. 'I beg your pardon, a slip of the tongue, I meant to say, your fork.' He reached down and recovered it and then held it tantalisingly above her head.

Enough was enough! She bounced to her feet and snatched it from him, her embarrassment replaced by annoyance. 'I have quite lost my appetite, your grace, I believe it to be the unpleasant company I'm keeping.' She was standing with one hand holding her ruined skirt together and the other waving an item of cutlery when Lady Harriet bustled in.

'Heavens above! Exactly what am I disturbing here?'

Charity dropped the fork and ran from the room. If the duke was as quick-witted as she believed, he would no doubt come up with a logical explanation for their extraordinary behaviour. She dashed through the house and back to her apartment expecting to find her cousin waiting to cross-examine her.

The sitting room was deserted; Patience must be in the bedchamber. She rushed in to find this empty also. She rang the bell vigorously and Sally appeared at once. 'Where is my cousin? I thought her to be resting here.'

'No, my lady, she has gone back to Essex. Mary and two chambermaids packed her trunks and your carriage came round and Miss Lawson left no more than a quarter of an hour ago.' The girl was gaping at her burned gown.

'I know, foolishly I got too close to the fire. Quickly, help me to put on something fresh, I must go down at once and tell his grace what has transpired.'

In record time she was in an elegant promenade dress, fresh petticoats and stockings and indoor slippers. Whilst she was dressing Charity warned her maid she might well be going out and she was to be ready to accompany her.

She flew through the house, skidded across the vestibule and erupted into the drawing room. The duke shot to his feet and Lady Harriet shook her head in dismay.

'Your grace, my cousin has run away. She told my maid she was returning to Essex but I fear this is not the case. I think she has eloped with Mr Pettigrew.'

8

Lady Harriet clutched her bosom and appeared to swoon. Charity was about to rush to her aid but the duke shook his head. 'Aunt Harry is perfectly well, but if we do not move fast I cannot say the same for Miss Lawson. We must go after her at once, you must come with me and bring your maid. Be ready to leave within half an hour.'

He didn't wait for her agreement but surged towards her and when she didn't move he lifted her to one side and left the building at a run. Was now the time to reveal that she had been impersonating her cousin these past few days? Lady Harriet looked decidedly unwell on hearing that a vicar's daughter had run away — goodness knew what her reaction would be if she were to understand the true circumstances.

'My lady, forgive me but I must do as the duke commands. If we cannot find my cousin before news of her disappearance becomes known her reputation will be in tatters.'

'Mr Pettigrew? Do you know this man? I understood your cousin to be a well-behaved young lady, I was sadly deceived on this point.' She warmed to her theme. 'I sincerely regret my offer to accommodate you and your cousin for the Season. When Miss Lawson is recovered I wish you both to leave Hanover Square.'

'I quite understand, my lady. I, too, wish we had not come to London.' Something else occurred to her that would not improve the situation. 'You have ordered a prodigious amount of gowns for us — what is to become of those?'

The redoubtable lady smiled. 'I shall send them on to you — they are of no use to me — and no doubt you can bedazzle the provincial gentlemen with your London finery. Think of them as a parting gift.'

Charity curtsied and ran back to her apartment. 'Sally, can you pack an overnight bag for each of us? You must do it quickly as the duke will be back to collect us very shortly.'

They were ready with moments to spare. She had changed her indoor slippers for her boots and found a warm scarf and mittens to take with her. A footman had appeared to carry their bags and today she took Sally down the main staircase, ignoring protocol.

The carriage was outside and the steps were down, however the duke was not inside. He had decided to ride despite the deteriorating weather. He was unrecognisable hidden under his many-caped riding coat and with a dark muffler wrapped around the lower part of his face. His beaver was pulled low on his brow.

'Hurry up, they have a considerable start on us, and we must catch them before they take accommodation for the night.'

She scrambled into the coach, delighted to find warm bricks and thick fur rugs had been provided for her comfort. As the door slammed behind her the first flakes of snow began to fall. She'd no time to enquire how he knew which direction Patience had taken; he was a resourceful man and she trusted him to know what he was doing. The fact that he had chosen to ride, and not travel inside with her, meant he was well aware of the difficulties that would be caused if they were to be in a closed carriage together even with her maid in attendance.

The coach rocked alarmingly as the team was pushed into a spanking trot. Travelling at speed over the cobbles was not a pleasant experience and she hoped Sally would not be unwell. There was no danger of her casting up her accounts as she had eaten nothing so far today. She thought longingly of the delicious array of food that she'd abandoned earlier.

With her feet on the bricks and the

rugs tucked around her knees she was warm but was extremely hungry. She would just have to ignore the rumblings of her insides and concentrate on the matter in hand. What had possessed her cousin to run away like this? As far as she knew, Patience had only known the wretched Pettigrew a few days — how could she believe she was in love with him? Unexpectedly an image of the duke passed through Charity's head and she pushed it aside.

The runaways could not marry without parental consent and even when Patience reached her majority she would still not have access to her inheritance as her trust fund did not mature until she was five and twenty. It didn't make sense. Why would she risk her reputation? There must be more to this romance than her cousin had divulged. Was Pettigrew not a fortune hunter but had fallen under her cousin's spell and was prepared to sacrifice everything to be with her?

A sudden hammering on the window

shocked her awake. The duke was riding alongside and gestured for her to open it. When she did so a blast of icy air and a flurry of snowflakes engulfed her.

'I sent men to make enquiries and I now am certain the errant couple are heading north.'

'Do you really think they are foolish enough to believe a Gretna Green marriage is valid in England?'

'I can think of no other reason they would travel in this direction. We must press on until we catch up with them.' Then, to her consternation, he reached down, swung the door wide open and tumbled from his saddle to land in a heap at her feet. Whoever he had handed the reins of his horse to slammed the door shut behind him. Before she could protest about his unorthodox entry he rolled to his feet and settled onto the squabs opposite her.

'I apologise for startling you, but I need to speak to you urgently about another matter. This morning I said I came to find you because I had news — in fact it is the very absence of news that makes the whole situation with the baby so extraordinary.'

Sally had shuffled into the far corner of the carriage and pulled the rug over her head as if by rendering herself invisible they could pretend they were alone.

'I take it from the cryptic comment, your grace, you have made no progress with your enquiries.'

'What I can tell you, my dear, is that Richard was not removed from any household within five miles of Green Park. There must be a good reason for his having been abandoned as he was, but I must admit I have not fathomed it.'

'We decided he could not have been in that thicket for more than an hour or two, which means whoever put him there did so in the dark. If they arrived on horseback or in a vehicle of some sort, they could have come from the countryside. You must widen the search soon as you return.' She stopped and shook her head. 'Unfortunately your aunt wishes both my cousin and me to return to Essex immediately so I can no longer help you with this matter.'

'I can see no problem — you can live at St James's Square. No, sweetheart, do not poker up, I'm not suggesting you reside at a bachelor establishment. I shall persuade my sister and her husband to join us.'

He leaned back and stretched his legs into the far corner. 'You have not opened the hamper. I thought you would be hungry so had my cook pack up a picnic for you.'

Her spirits lifted at the thought of sustenance. 'I didn't know there was one, your grace. I should certainly like something to eat as I have had nothing since supper last night.'

He delved under the seat and pulled out a wicker hamper. He unbuckled the straps and threw the lid open to reveal meat pasties, slices of plum cake, hard-boiled eggs and bread and cheese.

There was also a glass stoppered bottle containing what looked like elderflower cordial.

Charity addressed the bundle in the corner. 'Sally, are you hungry? There is plenty here for all of us.' A muffled voice replied that it had eaten a short while ago.

They tucked in and despite the constant jolting she managed not to spill anything or drop it in her lap. When the hamper was empty he pushed the napkins, glasses and other debris inside, deftly rebuckled it and rammed it under the seat.

'If you will excuse me, I shall resume my place outside.' He flung open the carriage door and in seconds resembled a snowman. 'Devil take it! We cannot continue in this weather.' He yelled into the blizzard. 'Stop at the next inn, it doesn't matter how poor it is, we have to get out of the snow.' His words were whipped away but his coachman thumped on the roof of the carriage indicating he understood.

The interior of the vehicle was decidedly unpleasant, even the rugs and bricks offered no protection against the arctic weather. He pulled the door closed and shook himself like an enormous canine, covering her with snow in the process.

She held her tongue until he'd folded himself into a corner. 'Look at me, your grace, I am wetter than you. I shall catch a putrid sore throat if I am obliged to remain as I am.'

He grinned, quite unrepentant. 'I'm sure you heard me instruct my coachmen to pull into the next hostelry. We are barely out of London, this is a toll road and there will be a decent coaching inn we can remain at until the weather improves.'

'There is a blizzard outside — we might be marooned for days. My cousin will be ruined if we don't remove her from Mr Pettigrew before nightfall.'

His expression changed. 'Think about it, my dear, they will be unable to travel. As soon as we can move again we will overtake them. Miss Lawson has her maid with her so that should be enough to protect her name. She is travelling in her family coach, not a hired vehicle, which also makes matters easier.'

'I sincerely hope that is correct, my aunt and uncle will be devastated if she succeeds in her plan. Whatever happens, sir, I intend to return to the country. Coming to London was a mistake and I wish I hadn't agreed to accompany my cousin.'

No sooner had she spoken than she realised she was speaking as herself and not as her cousin would have. Too late to retract the words — she would explain everything to him when they were private.

She daren't look at him and see his condemnation, so closed her eyes and pretended to sleep. Minutes later the coach lurched sideways and there were lights outside in the snow. Thank goodness! They had turned into a coaching house and she would be able to change into something drier and Sally could emerge from her cocoon.

He was out of the coach the moment it rocked to a standstill. He flung the steps down himself and then without a by your leave reached in and snatched her from the seat, leaving Sally to find her own way. He enveloped her with his riding coat and strode through the whiteness and into the welcome warmth of the inn.

He put her on her feet. 'Remain here, I shall organise chambers for us.'

She stood in a growing puddle of melting snow, sure he had guessed her secret. She wished she had told him herself, he would have been less angry at her deception if she had been honest with him.

The front door crashed open a second time and a snow-covered coachman staggered in with Sally in his arms. He was followed by another groom with their baggage. After such a dramatic entrance she expected the reception area to be full of interested spectators, but only a portly landlord was there to see them.

'I bid you welcome, my lord, I reckon

141

you're after rooms for the night. You're lucky, the mail coach hasn't arrived and there are plenty of good chambers available.'

'I wish for a chamber for my ward and her maid and one for myself. I shall also need rooms for my staff and stabling for my horses.'

'At once, my lord, I will have you shown directly to them. Would you be requiring refreshments taken to your rooms?'

'Nothing at the moment, but we will require supper to be served in a private parlour at five o'clock.'

The landlord nodded and beckoned to a couple of girls who were lurking in the shadows. 'Show these fine people to the apartments at the rear of the house. Then take up hot water and anything else that they might require. Hurry up now, don't stand around gawping.'

The rooms Charity was shown to were more than adequate — in fact they were of a far higher standard than her own modest bedroom at the vicarage. There was already a substantial fire burning in the large grate and the room was delightfully warm after the perishing conditions outside.

Charity prayed her cousin had found safety somewhere on the road even if by so doing she would lose her good name. The duke had not said anything about visiting her up here so she would have to go to him. She had no wish to discuss something so disgraceful in front of Sally.

The inn was all but empty of customers, there would be nobody here to relay gossip to anyone that mattered. The duke had not given his real name so with luck they could both remain anonymous. As long as Lady Harriet did not divulge their whereabouts all might yet be smoothed over. The blizzard was a godsend and should keep everybody at home — the musical evening they had been expected to attend would be cancelled and nobody need know both she and her cousin had been gallivanting across the country in a most unseemly way.

Her gown was unharmed by the

snow and her cloak would soon dry in front of the fire. 'I must speak to the duke, Sally, I shall not be above a few minutes.'

The passageway outside was quiet — indeed, the entire building was eerily silent. He had been given the apartment opposite hers so she stepped boldly across and knocked overloudly on the door.

★ ★ ★

Hugo had not brought his valet but he found this no inconvenience as he was well used to taking care of himself. He draped his riding coat over the back of the chair and pushed it in front of the fire where it began to steam gently. He found a rack and cleaned the worst of the mud and snow from his boots and then checked that the rest of his garments would pass muster.

For some reason he wanted to look his best for the forthcoming interview with the girl he was head over heels in love with. His chest felt tight and he had the urge to laugh out loud — something he was not accustomed to do. Falling in love so quickly was quite out of character, but he didn't regret it for one instant. She was the perfect wife for him — not only was she beautiful, kind and intelligent, she was also an heiress and would solve his financial problems at one go.

He patted his pocket; he had a betrothal ring in his waistcoat and intended to ask her to marry him this very afternoon. He had deliberately addressed her in such a way that her maid would be well aware there was more between them than friendship — although he hoped his future wife also considered herself his friend.

There were no other young ladies of his acquaintance he would wish to spend the rest of his life with. He frowned as he remembered her strange comment about the reason she had come to London. For all that Miss Lawson was from humble stock, it would appear she had been instrumental in persuading Patience to accept Aunt Harry's offer. No doubt this was because she was already planning to elope with Pettigrew and would find it far easier to do so from Town than from a village in Essex.

Did his beloved reciprocate his feelings? He was almost sure she did, but until he made her an offer and gauged her response, he could not be entirely confident. He hoped that his elevated status would persuade her parents to give their consent as, after all, she was unlikely to receive a better offer. He might be short of funds, but he was the only duke on the marriage mart at present.

He pushed the worry of Miss Lawson firmly to the back of his mind; also the conundrum of Richard's missing parents, for there was nothing he could do about either of these with a blizzard blowing outside. However, he could use their enforced stay at this hostelry to his advantage and convince her he would make an excellent husband.

A loud knock on the door startled him out of his romantic reverie. He snatched the door open to discover to his delight his future wife was standing outside the door. 'Come in, sweetheart, I was just thinking about you.' He deliberately closed the door behind them — if she believed she was compromised perhaps she would feel obligated to accept his offer of marriage, especially if he reminded her that her cousin was already beyond the pale. 'I was about to come and see you as there is something I must say to you and I believe you know what it is.'

She looked relieved at his words. 'Your grace, please say what you must.'

He couldn't prevent the surge of heat that travelled to his nether regions. He had not expected her to come to him, but he was delighted that she had. In his excitement at the prospect of having the girl he loved to distraction return his feelings, he didn't stop to consider how out of character it was for a young lady of good breeding to have visited him without her maid.

His happiness made him giddy. He swept her into his arms and tilted her face so he had access to her lips. She tasted as sweet as he'd expected and after a moment's hesitation, her mouth softened beneath his and she returned his kiss.

When he raised his head he was overjoyed to see his love reflected in her lovely face. 'My darling, I am in love with you but I hardly dared hope you shared my feelings. Will you make me the happiest of men and consent to be my duchess?'

9

Charity had been so surprised by his embrace that she hadn't struggled or protested. For a few heady seconds she was transported to a world full of pleasure and possibilities and then he added to her happiness by asking her to marry him.

Her feet were still dangling in mid-air and the heat of his body was burning through her gown. She didn't hesitate. She must have misunderstood his position and he had decided to marry for love and not for convenience. 'I cannot believe we have reached this stage after knowing each other for less than a week. If you are quite sure you wish to marry me, knowing what you do, then I am delighted to accept.'

He kissed her again and she responded loving the feel of his mouth against hers, the way he stroked her hair and how his heart was pounding against hers. Eventually he released her and strangely turned his back.

His voice was gruff when he spoke to her. 'I apologise for taking disgraceful advantage of you, my darling, but you are so beautiful I could not resist. You must go now, I will write at once to your parents and to my aunt with the good news. I don't give a damn how bad the weather is, my stallion can make it back to London.'

'I love you, I am so happy I could burst. I only wish that my cousin is as happy with her choice as I am with mine.'

She ran from the room and across the narrow passageway into her own chamber. She couldn't help herself from bursting out with her news. 'The duke has asked me to marry him, Sally, and I have accepted.'

The girl beamed and curtsied. 'Congratulations, my lady, you will make a perfect duchess.'

Charity realised there were still loose ends to tie before her deception could be put to one side. She would speak to her future husband and let him decide if they should maintain the pretence whilst in London. Of course, his aunt would be aware, but she was hardly likely to pass this information on to her cronies as it would reflect badly on herself. Thank goodness she and Patience had not actually attended any functions.

She could hardly credit that two sensible people had managed to fall so hopelessly in love after spending so little time together. She flung herself on the bed to think about her future life. Never in her wildest dreams had she imagined she might be so elevated — her parents would be overjoyed. Not because she was marrying a duke, but because she had found a gentleman she wished to spend the rest of her life with. He had not talked of when they were to be married, she would ask him if they could wait at least until the summer so she could get to know him better and discover exactly what her duties as his wife would be.

Why had Patience run away so unexpectedly? It didn't make sense — if she truly loved Mr Pettigrew then her parents would eventually have agreed to her marriage. They might have made her wait a year to see if her feelings were truly engaged, but they would never do anything to make their oldest daughter unhappy. Her cousin's disappearance was another thing to add to the extraordinary events of the past few days.

Until she had come to Town her life had been relatively uneventful, but since her arrival she had rescued a baby, fallen in love and become engaged to the most wonderful man in the world. She would marry him even if he were a pauper — in fact she would prefer it if he were a commoner; then she would not feel so out of her depth.

The duke had told her to return to her room, but she should have insisted they discuss matters in more detail. She would leave him to complete his letters and then send Sally to ask him to join her. She was too restless to remain on the bed. She must find writing materials.

'Sally, please take a message to his grace. Tell him I am also writing a letter to my parents and would like him to put it in with his. I can see there's paper and ink on the bureau so I should have it completed within ten minutes.'

As she had no idea where she was she could hardly put the address on the top of her letter. Instead she wrote a brief note saying that she had accepted an offer of marriage from The Duke of Edbury and he was writing to them. She apologised for not having followed the usual procedure, but assured them she was delighted with the match.

She sanded the note and folded it neatly and sealed it with a blob of wax melted by the candle flame. Then she reversed the letter and addressed it to her father.

'Here you are, Sally, I am done. Please take it, as no doubt his grace is waiting for it.'

* * *

Hugo had just completed a letter to his aunt when he heard a knock on the door which must herald the arrival of the missive to be included with his own. He strode to the door and took the letter from the maid. He had already sent down a message to warn the head coachman to select someone to brave the weather and return to London with the letters. Aunt Harry could send on the two for the earl.

He rang the bell to summon a servant and collected the two he'd written. He saw the names on the one from his beloved. His fists clenched and he was obliged to put out his hand to support himself.

Suddenly things that had bothered him were explained. He staggered to the bed and collapsed on it, unable to think clearly. For some reason the cousins had exchanged places and he had just offered to marry Miss Lawson not Lady Patience.

This catastrophe was not entirely her fault — she had come to tell him who she was; had mistakenly believed he knew. She had revealed her true identity by her comment in the carriage but he had failed to pick up on it. Then she had expressed her surprise that he had made her an offer and still he had not understood the references.

He had been so blinded by his infatuation he was now irrevocably committed to marrying the most unsuitable bride. He should immediately storm into her room and accuse her of deceiving him and cut the connection, but he couldn't do it.

He could not break her heart after making her so happy.

He rubbed his eyes. His finances were in desperate straits. If he didn't marry an heiress this year he would lose his principal estates and be forced to eke out his existence in Northumbria. If he had known the real circumstances he would have kept his feelings to himself, given up any hope of true happiness, and married for convenience and not love.

How could he have ruined both their lives in such a foolhardy manner? Then something else, even more catastrophic, occurred to him. If Miss Lawson was with him, then the real heiress was being abducted by a fortune hunter. Not only had he failed himself, he had let down his aunt by not protecting her goddaughter. He looked at the letters scattered on the floor and thanked God that at least he hadn't had time to send them.

How was he going to handle this without causing unnecessary distress to Miss Lawson — no, in future she would be Charity to him. He must speak to her at once, but say what exactly? He was just deciding how to handle the situation when the door flew open and she rushed in.

He kicked the letters under the bed

and stood up, finding it far easier to greet her with a smile than he'd expected. 'Sweetheart, what is it? Why are you in such a pother?'

'Your grace, we cannot remain here in comfort when Patience could be in the hands of a fortune hunter. We have allowed our happiness to cloud our judgement. I have been thinking about what she told me and can see no reason why my uncle would refuse to allow her to marry him. She said he was the eldest son of Sir John Pettigrew, not wealthy perhaps, but well-bred enough to satisfy her parents, surely?'

'I sent one of my men ahead to make enquiries, I'm hoping he will still be able to return before dark.'

'There's no reason to send to my parents or your aunt immediately — could you not use that groom to continue the search?'

'An excellent idea, sweetheart, but there's no point in doing so until I've heard from the man I sent earlier.'

'My head is all over the place, I can't

think straight. Too much has happened in the past few days.' For some reason she hovered in the doorway and didn't come in. 'I have been considering your offer, and have decided on reflection to refuse it. We have rushed into this and until Patience is found, and Richard returned to his parents, I cannot think about anything else.' She paused and seemed to have difficulty swallowing. 'We were carried away and said things we didn't really mean. I might be naive, but I do recognise the difference between love and desire. I believe it is the latter that prompted your offer.'

He stared at her open-mouthed, unable to believe she had just released him from his promise. Far from being overjoyed at his lucky escape he realised in that moment that he would rather be married to Charity and live in the northern wilds, than marry another girl, save his estates and live in luxury.

★ ★ ★

'I know you are somewhat surprised, your grace, as we have both declared our love for each other. Therefore, if you still feel the same way in a few months' time then come and speak to my father. I cannot promise you I will have changed my mind, but you are welcome to ask the question a second time.

'Whatever the outcome of the next few days, I shall return to Essex, I am not comfortable in London.' She was finding it increasingly difficult to continue, but she had come in to tell him she didn't wish to marry him and must do so.

'There is another reason for my refusal, I would not make you a suitable duchess. Love is all very well, sir, but I feel that neither of us would be happy in this match. You require an heiress and I do not wish to get married at all.'

Before he could reply she stepped backwards, closed his door and was safely inside her own chamber with the door firmly bolted. Her speech to him had been the hardest thing she had ever done in her life. She loved him, would always do so, but she was not the one for him. Aristocrats should marry someone from their own class, or failing that a girl with a substantial fortune. She did not qualify on either count and would not allow him to throw away his heritage on a whim.

He had fallen in love with Lady Patience, the eldest daughter of an earl with a massive fortune. If he had known her true identity he would not have given her a second thought. He knew his duty and she loved him too much to hold him to a promise he must have regretted the moment he'd spoken.

Her maid was staring at her as if she had run mad — time to explain the deception to her abigail. 'Therefore, Sally, you must refer to me in future as Miss Lawson. Also, you must never speak of what took place here. I was never betrothed and certainly not to The Duke of Edbury.'

Instead of looking horrified the girl

looked relieved. 'That explains every-thing, Miss Lawson. I've been at my wits' end trying to make head or tail of what Mary told me. Now it all makes sense.'

The thunderous knocking on the door interrupted their conversation. 'Miss Lawson, I demand that you open this door at once. I must speak with you immediately.'

Charity shook her head and ran into the bedchamber, closely followed by her maid, and slammed the door and pushed the bolt across firmly. She couldn't hear the banging from here and hoped he would have the sense to desist before he roused the entire building and they came to investigate.

There was no external door so the duke could not get to her in here. She had done the right thing but it had broken her heart to do so and she wouldn't take much persuading to change her mind if he was face-to-face with her.

'Sally, tell me at once what you know

about Lady Patience and Mr Pettigrew.'

'Mary was always with her ladyship, she never left her alone with the gentleman. I believe they forgot she was there most of the time and talked freely in front of her.'

'Mary should not have told you what she heard, but as she was the one to break the confidence you can have no qualms about revealing everything she said to me.'

'It's like this, miss. It would seem that Lady Patience had been meeting the gentleman in secret for some time. Only after their affections were engaged did they discover that the earl had a falling out with Sir John Pettigrew many years ago and they are still at daggers drawn. That's why they decided to run away together.'

'My uncle dotes on my cousin, he would never let his personal feelings ruin his daughter's happiness. It still doesn't make sense. Think, Sally, you must tell me anything that Mary said to you on the subject.'

The duke was *in loco parentis* and despite her reservations about seeing him it was her duty to tell him everything, but first she would elicit every scrap of information from her maid.

Sally was wringing her hands. 'I've just remembered something, miss. It didn't mean anything to me at the time, but now I fear what Mary overheard makes Mr Pettigrew a villain and not the gentleman I thought him to be.'

'Well, what is it? We cannot help Lady Patience if we do not know the truth.'

'It was that time we went to the menagerie and Mary was sent with a message. She arrived before the appointed time and waited in the shelter of a doorway. The gentleman in question stopped right in front of her, he was deep in conversation with a common person. She hadn't meant to eavesdrop.'

'Never mind that, what did she hear?'

'That Mr Pettigrew handed the other man a bag of coins and told him to be ready when he got the message. Mary only mentioned it in passing, we had a right old laugh thinking the gentlemen were involved in gambling or some such — but now I reckon they were arranging the abduction.'

'Lady Patience left of her own free will, she was not abducted, she took her maid and her trunks with her. However, there is something decidedly havey-cavey about all this and I must give this information at once to the duke. He will know what to do.'

She hastened to the door and threw the bolt across and shivered. Why was the room so cold and how did there come to be snow on the carpet? A figure stepped from shadows by the window and she screamed.

'I beg your pardon, I did not mean to startle you, Miss Lawson, I was obliged to climb the ivy outside your sitting room window in order to gain access.' Hugo calmly brushed the snow from his shoulders and perched on the windowsill in order to pull his boots back on. She hadn't noticed he was in his stockinged feet until that moment.

He didn't look angry nor particularly upset. In fact, if she was honest, he looked more irritated than anything else.

'Believe it or not, sir, I was just coming to speak to you.' She couldn't stop the gurgle of mirth escaping. 'I'm sorry you had to brave the elements in such a dramatic fashion, but am relieved you didn't kick the door down.' She gestured towards an armchair on the right of the fire and sat opposite and waited whilst he settled.

She then regaled him with all that Sally had told her, glad she could pass the knowledge on to someone else and not have the responsibility for making any decisions on the matter. He listened without comment, apparently relaxed, and when she completed her story he nodded.

'It's as I thought, my dear, whoever this bastard is, he certainly isn't a gentleman with honourable intentions. His was a deliberate ploy to gain your cousin's affections and then entice her to run away with him with more lies. I doubt his name is even Pettigrew. Everything he told Lady Patience was untrue.'

How could they be sitting here calmly discussing these things when her beloved cousin was in such mortal danger? She jumped to her feet so fast her chair crashed to the floor. 'I refuse to sit here in comfort a moment longer. I insist that we set out immediately and find Patience before . . . before — ' She couldn't continue, couldn't speak out loud what she was thinking.

He was beside her before she could move back. She tried to snatch her hands away but he held them firmly. His calmness, his strength, flowed into her and her heart stopped pounding and her vision cleared.

'Miss Lawson, I give you my word as a gentleman that I will recover Lady Patience and return her to her parents. Do you trust me?' She nodded. 'Then all will be well. My man discovered that a carriage containing a man and two young ladies tipped over not a mile from here. The occupants have taken shelter at a farmhouse and I shall go at once to recover your cousin.'

'Can you use your carriage in the snow?'

'No, I shall go on horseback. It will be an uncomfortable and cold ride but no more than she deserves.' His face hardened and for a moment he looked terrifying. 'I shall deal with her abductor first, so do not expect me back immediately.'

He released her and smiled. 'Don't look so worried, little one, I shall come to no harm.'

She smiled back. 'I was not worried on your behalf, your grace, but I beg you not to kill Mr Pettigrew. I believe that even a duke can be hung by the neck if he commits murder.'

He laughed out loud and gently flicked her cheek with his finger. He glanced over her shoulder. 'Take care of your mistress. You did well to pass on this information, Sally.' Then he headed for the door, turning at the last minute to speak again. 'You are an original, my love, do not think I shall let you go so easily.'

10

Hugo closed the door behind him still smiling. Whatever his beloved might think was the case, as far as he was concerned they were still betrothed and would be married at the end of the Season. They would not be exactly penniless, the estate in the north would support a family in moderate comfort. Charity was a vicar's daughter, she was used to living a simple life so it would be no hardship for her.

He threw on his riding coat, grabbed his gloves and beaver, tied a warm muffler around his face and he was ready to go. He'd already sent word to the stables to have his stallion ready and he had taken the precaution of asking for a rug to be thrown over the beast's rump to protect him from the elements.

The landlord waylaid him on his way out. 'My lord, would you still be wanting your room tonight? Are the young lady and her maid remaining behind?'

Hugo fixed him with a disdainful stare. 'Remember your place. The rooms are paid for — go about your business.'

The man nodded and bowed and slunk away and Hugo regretted his bad temper. The man was only looking after his interests. The weather was improving and no doubt further weary travellers would arrive demanding accommodation for the night; it was only logical the landlord would wish to know if they were vacating their rooms for some reason. He would smooth things over when he returned.

He cursed at his maladroit handling of the situation. He would be bringing Lady Patience back to the inn and now he had antagonised the owner, the man was unlikely to remain discreet about what he saw.

The snow had settled and was no longer swirling about making visibility difficult, but unfortunately, it being late afternoon, it was almost dark. His two men, mounted on sturdy hunters, and his stallion were waiting in the yard.

'I shall bring back Lady Patience, Jones, and you will transport the girl. Remember not to use any names when we are at the farm. Hopefully, Lady Patience had the sense to travel incognito.'

They hadn't discussed how they would deal with Pettigrew and his henchmen. He patted his pocket, checking he'd got his loaded pistols. His men carried stout cudgels and knew how to use them.

After a ride of no more than a quarter of an hour he saw the upturned carriage and recognised it as the one that the girls had arrived in last week. He then spied the farm buildings set back from the road a few yards. What a pity they had not continued their journey as they would have come across the upturned vehicle and been able to effect a rescue immediately.

He raised his hand and beckoned his

men closer. 'We will dismount here. Jones, you hold on to the animals and Trent and I will go on foot and deal with any men left outside.' They nodded and he continued. 'As soon as I give you the word, bring the horses in and find somewhere warm for them. It shouldn't take long to collect Lady Patience and her maid, but you never know, the chit might refuse to come. It's perfectly possible she still believes Pettigrew to be a man of honour.'

He removed his pistols from his pocket and checked they were primed and loaded. He sincerely hoped he wouldn't have to use either of them, but better to be prepared than not. The snow underfoot deadened his footsteps and he moved stealthily forwards until he heard rough male voices coming from just ahead of him. He raised his arm and Trent slithered to a halt behind him.

'I ain't hanging about out here much longer, Jim, it ain't worth the few shillings what you gave me.'

A second man replied. 'Quit your moaning, we ain't going nowhere until the farmer gets off his arse and helps pull the carriage out the ditch.' There was a deal of coughing and spitting and then the man resumed. 'We was promised five guineas when he's sure the girl will marry him. It'll be full dark soon, them grand folk don't hold with their young ladies staying out all night with a gen'leman. I reckon as we'll be paid right enough in a day or two.'

'But the cove ain't conscious, he could kick the bucket and then we'll get nothing.'

These were the villains Hugo was searching for. He removed his pistols, cocked them and stepped around the edge of the building. 'Put your hands above your head. Do it now.'

Both men did as he bid, so startled by his sudden appearance they had no time to attempt a retaliation. 'Tie them up, Trent, and toss them in a shed where the magistrate can find them in the morning.' He handed his man a pistol. He didn't need to wait to see if his instructions would be followed, his men were loyal and efficient in their duties.

The path to the farmhouse was easy to discern because of the footprints showing black in the snow. He had no wish to frighten the farmer or his wife so hastily shoved his weapon into his pocket. He was forced to bend his knees in order to hammer on the door; he wanted the occupants to be in no doubt that someone in authority wished to come in.

Brisk footsteps approached and the door was pulled open without hesitation. A sprightly lady of middle years, dressed for warmth rather than fashion, her hair covered by a snowy-white cap, curtsied politely.

'Good afternoon, your grace, we were expecting you to come and rescue your ward.' She stepped aside and waved him in.

What on earth had possessed Patience to reveal both their identities like this? Was she determined to ruin her reputation completely? He unbuttoned his riding coat and swung it from his shoulders in one movement, then shook it vigorously and hung it on a convenient peg by the door.

For once he was lost for words. Until he'd spoken to the girl he had no idea what Banbury tale she'd spun to these good folks. The farmer's wife spoke from behind him. 'Lady Patience explained that your man of business was escorting her to visit with relatives in Watford. I'm sorry to tell you, your grace, that the poor man is still unconscious from the fall he took when the carriage overturned.'

'Most unfortunate, madam, I shall have him collected as soon as the roads are clear and recompense you for your trouble.'

She seemed pleased at his statement and he guessed times were hard for small tenant farmers such as these. She pointed to a room to the left of the flagstone passageway. 'Her ladyship and her maid suffered no serious injury, they are warm and dry in my front parlour and eagerly awaiting your arrival.'

'Thank you, I shall also collect the baggage as soon as possible.' God knew how he was going to explain the two villains trussed up like turkeys in the shed outside. And what the hell had happened to the original coachman and the groom?

He hoped they had not come to an untimely end.

He would get Trent to turn these two loose, no doubt they would be only too pleased to escape the noose for their part in this abduction.

He knocked on the door but didn't wait to be asked to enter. He stepped in, not sure what to expect. He was almost floored as Patience threw herself into his arms and burst into noisy tears. He patted her on the back and said what was appropriate and waited for her to recover her composure. Eventually she sniffed to a halt and he offered her his handkerchief.

'Thank you, your grace, for this and

for coming to my rescue. I have made the most dreadful mistake and just pray that my poor parents and my siblings will not be obliged to share in my disgrace.'

He gently untangled her from his jacket and guided her to a wooden settle placed by the fire. Immediately her abigail took charge giving him time to decide what best to say in this difficult situation. 'Lady Patience, we have much to talk about but here is not the place. I have come to take you to your cousin who is nearby at a coaching inn. Unfortunately, you will be forced to ride pillion with me, and your girl will have to travel in similar fashion with my man. Please get your cloaks on immediately, the sooner you are safely away from here the better.'

He delved into his pocket and found several golden guineas. He hoped this would be enough to buy these simple folk's silence. 'Be outside in five minutes.'

There had been no sign of the farmer

but he could hear movement in the kitchen and knocked politely on the door. When it was pulled open he dropped the coins into her outstretched hand. 'If you will continue to take care of my man until I can have him collected, I should be most grateful. Also your discretion in this matter would be appreciated.' The implication was clear. There would be more gold forthcoming if she was prepared to hold her tongue about the incident.

The woman bobbed. 'My husband will take care of your horses and repair the carriage as soon as he can pull it out of the ditch. He's off fetching the apothecary to take a look at the invalid. I'll settle the bill for his services, your grace, from the gold you've given me.'

He nodded graciously. 'Thank you, someone will be back in a day or two and will settle any outstanding remu-nerations.' He headed for the front door, collected his coat, and marched around to the outbuildings where he found his men and his horses sheltering in an open barn.

'Release the men in the shed, Trent, I don't want them contradicting the story Lady Patience has told.' He quickly explained how things were and they understood immediately. The two miscreants vanished into the darkness not a moment too soon as the front door to the farmhouse opened a second time and the farmer's wife appeared with Patience and her maid.

'Come along, we must be away immediately or it will be too dark to ride.' As soon as his ward arrived at his side he snatched her up and tossed her in front of his saddle, then vaulted on behind her. He pulled his coat around her, glad that it was so voluminous. He put one arm about her waist, clicked his tongue and his stallion moved away smoothly. They would be back at the inn long before the animal became tired under the double burden.

The girl pressed herself against him and swayed in time with the horse — she was obviously an excellent horsewoman. 'Hang on, my lady, we shall canter the rest of the way.'

* * *

Charity needed something to occupy her time whilst she waited for the duke to return with her cousin. She turned to Sally. 'Lady Patience will be sharing with me and I doubt she will have her luggage with her tonight. One of us will have to sleep in our petticoats. Do I have a spare gown she can use tomorrow?'

'You do, Miss Lawson, I was able to put in two spare as well as clean petticoats and stockings. Do you wish me to organise things for her arrival?'

'Yes, do so at once. You must also have them bring up another truckle bed for Mary; you can put them up in the sitting room once Lady Patience and I have retired. Whilst you're downstairs, would you be so kind as to order supper for two, to be served up here?'

'Immediately, miss, and I'll arrange

for hot water to be brought as well.' She paused as if thinking about her next question. 'Will we be going back to Essex as soon as we return to Town? I couldn't help but overhear you saying you no longer wish to stay for the Season.'

This was the most unsuitable conversation to be having with her maid but Sally made a valid point. Whatever she and Patience did then their abigails must do the same. 'I think it might be best if we did, but I shall keep an open mind on the subject until I have discussed it with my cousin. That said, I'm sure Lady Harriet will no longer wish to have us living under her roof after the events of the past twenty-four hours.'

The girl seemed satisfied with that, dropped a small curtsy, and disappeared into the bedchamber where she could be heard organising matters so that they could all sleep comfortably. A short while later she slipped through the sitting room and out into the corridor to take the various messages to the kitchen.

How long would it take to rescue Patience? Hugo had been gone an hour already, so maybe her cousin was safe and on her way to the inn. She checked that the bedchamber was ready, that there was a good fire burning in the grate and then returned to the sitting room. Sally had drawn the curtains earlier to keep the heat in, but Charity needed to know if the weather had improved. She stepped behind the curtain and pressed her nose to the glass.

Darkness had fallen and she could see nothing at all through the small panes. The window didn't have a latch which was why he had been able to get in so easily. She pushed, but it didn't budge. Maybe her shoulder would work better than her hand. She drew the curtain back so she could take a run at it and charged. The force of her arrival opened the window so suddenly she almost went headfirst into the yard below.

An avalanche of snow shot off the roof and she was engulfed before she had time to withdraw her head. She stepped away and shook herself in an attempt to remove the nasty white stuff. At least she knew it was no longer snowing, which had been the main reason for opening the window. As she leaned out to pull it closed she heard horses rapidly approaching.

The duke clattered into the yard closely followed by a second horseman. At first she couldn't see her cousin, then a shrouded shape in front of the duke slithered to the ground.

'Patience, I'm so glad to see you,' she yelled, quite forgetting that a young lady was supposed to speak with a lowered voice at all times.

Her shout sent both horses skittering across the cobbles and Patience barely managed to skip out of the way before she was trampled underfoot. Charity hastily withdrew closing the window firmly behind her. From the fulminating glare she'd received she had not endeared herself to the hero of the hour.

She shivered in her wet gown and wished she had not been so foolish. Never mind, she would change and Sally could have this one dry for tomorrow. A sharp knock on the door sent her running to open it but instead of her cousin or the duke, it was Sally and a positive bevy of maids carrying water and supper trays.

'Excellent, you have arrived in good time. Sally, Lady Patience and his grace have arrived and will be here momentarily. As you can see I also need to change my gown; we shall do that first, and then have our meal.'

The cloth-covered trays smelled appetising and her stomach gurgled in anticipation. The three jugs of hot water should be more than ample to restore everyone's appearance. Before she could retreat Patience appeared at the end of the corridor and flew into her arms.

Her cousin was distraught, crying and talking simultaneously and making no sense. They really shouldn't be in the corridor making a spectacle of themselves but she was unable to move into the privacy of her sitting room.

The duke snatched Patience from her arms and carried her like a recalcitrant toddler into the sitting room so Charity was able to skip in hastily behind him. She was about to close the door when Mary hurried up. 'Come in, everything is ready. Sally is waiting to assist you with her ladyship.'

The duke put his burden down and pushed Charity none too gently towards the bedchamber, then he turned to her and shook his head. 'Devil take it! How the hell have you managed to be wetter than your cousin when you remained inside?'

She opened her mouth to explain but he raised his hand. 'That was a rhetorical question and I do not require you to speak. Also I did not appreciate you behaving like a fishwife and almost causing your cousin to be injured.'

He glared at her but, remembering

his previous remark, she made no reply. Unfortunately this was the incorrect response. 'Have you nothing to say for yourself, Miss Lawson?'

Charity decided she had had quite enough of being berated like a schoolgirl. She squared her shoulders and gave him stare for stare. 'I am wet, your grace, because snow from the roof fell on me whilst I was looking out of the window. How I conduct myself is none of your business, if I wish to behave like a fishwife I shall do so.' What in heaven's name had made her say something so ridiculous? She must make her escape whilst he was still trying to make sense of what she'd said.

He was standing by the fire and as a large lump of snow fell from his coat into the flames the coal hissed and spluttered, distracting him for a vital second. She fled past him and into the sanctuary of her bedchamber knowing he would not follow her there.

Why was it that every time they were together sparks flew and they were at daggers drawn? She was not fond of dictatorial, arrogant men — not that she knew any — and must suppose that her extraordinary pronouncement of undying love for the duke was a momentary infatuation. After all, had not her cousin been so afflicted and only now understood there had been no love involved on either side?

'Patience, you must tell me everything that has transpired whilst we are changing. And I have something extraordinary to tell you as well.'

11

When they eventually emerged, freshly gowned and more than ready for their supper, it was to find that both trays had vanished. Charity stared in astonishment at the empty tables.

'I cannot imagine where our meal has gone. There were two trays waiting for us on the sideboard and now they are gone.'

Patience called Mary. 'Kindly go down to the kitchen and enquire as to what has happened to our meal. If they have no notion, ask if we can have a second supper sent up to us at once.'

Charity went to see who or what was causing all the noise outside the window. 'Oh dear! The yard is full of carriages and the stagecoach has also just pulled in. I fear we are unlikely to get anything else given to us tonight.' She frowned and stared at the empty sideboard. 'I know where our food is. That wretched man has stolen our supper as a punishment. Wait here, I shall go immediately and demand he returns it.'

With her cousin at her heels she skipped across the passageway and banged on the door of the duke's apartment. After a few moments the door swung open and he leant nonchalantly in the doorway with a decidedly smug expression.

'You have our trays and I demand that you return them forthwith.'

He stepped to one side and pointed to the table by the fire. 'You may certainly have the trays, Miss Lawson, but there is precious little left to eat on either of them. The soup was quite delicious as were the meat pasties and fruitcake.' He was openly laughing at them and this was too much for her fragile temper.

Before he could take evasive action she bunched her fist and punched him in the face. Unprepared for her attack, he staggered backwards clutching his nose. Whilst he was unbalanced she jumped forward and shoved him hard in the chest, delighted to see him tumble backwards to land in an undignified heap on his derriere.

Seeing him flattened and bleeding almost made up for the agonising pain in the hand with which she'd made contact with his aristocratic nose. Then his bemused expression changed to incandescent rage.

'Quickly, into our rooms before he gets up.' She barely had time to slam the bolt across before his shoulder hit the door. His language made her ears burn and her cousin giggle nervously.

'He climbed in the window when I locked him out last time, we must make sure that it's fastened or he will be in here again.' She and Patience raced to the window and searched frantically for some way of keeping it closed.

'If we draw the curtains again and then place that wooden settle against the window I doubt he'd be able to open it from outside,' her cousin suggested helpfully.

They were struggling across the room with the item of furniture when Charity dropped her end, causing Patience to use a most unbecoming word. 'Mary is locked out — if we open the door to let her in then *he* will come in also.'

'I can't leave my girl outside in the passageway all night. Without her beside me things could have been so much worse.'

Sally cleared her throat. 'Excuse me, miss, but with all the racket outside I doubt that his grace will attempt to climb in your window again.'

'You're perfectly correct, we must return the settle to its original position. If you would assist us, Sally, I'm sure we will get it done far quicker.'

When the room was back as it should be, Charity crept across to the sitting room door and put her ear to the panel. 'I do believe he's gone, but he could be lurking outside and will pounce on me if I open the door to look for Mary.' She turned to her maid. 'Sally, exactly where do the back stairs emerge?'

'At the far end from the main staircase, miss, I reckon a bit further away from our room and the others.'

Patience flopped into an armchair and clutched her stomach pathetically. 'I am dying of starvation, Charity, I shall not survive until breakfast. I was too upset to eat today and have had nothing since yesterday supper time.'

There were half a dozen rooms in their corridor and from the loud voices and banging outside people were arriving to occupy them. She jumped to her feet and rushed to the door. 'The duke can hardly barge in here in front of other guests so I believe it will be perfectly safe to open the door. I pray Mary is already outside.'

Patience and Sally vanished into the bedchamber leaving her to face him alone. Despite the snow she'd rubbed on her bruised knuckles they had swollen and were an interesting shade of blue. She sincerely hoped she had not broken them — although it would be her just deserts if she had.

Cautiously she slid back the bolts and opened the door a fraction so she could peer out. An elegant lady in a bonnet festooned with fruit and birds was walking by accompanied by a gentleman who could only be her husband. They were being escorted by two servants from the inn. She opened the door and looked down the corridor, but there was no sign of the missing maid.

'How kind of you to let me in, Miss Lawson, I do so wish to speak to you in private.'

The duke had been waiting on the left of the door knowing she would look to the right. As two further guests were at the head of the stairs she could hardly slam the door in his face without drawing unwanted attention. How could she have been so stupid? Of course he had worked out the very same thing and used it to his advantage.

Her legs all but collapsed beneath her

and she was forced to grip the door frame in order to remain upright. Somehow she managed to reply and was pleased her voice emerged quite normally. 'In which case, your grace, you had better come in. Make sure that you leave the door wide open — we have no wish to offend the proprieties do we?'

Maybe with the door open she would be safe from physical retribution and he would have to speak quietly if he wasn't to be heard by those traversing the corridor. She walked to the fire and sat primly on the settle. She risked a glance at his face.

Instantly she was on her feet and by his side staring at him in horror at the damage she'd inflicted. 'I'm so sorry, I should not have struck you. Have I broken your nose? I fear you will have the most spectacular black eye by the morning.'

For a moment he remained silent and she could not read his expression. She had behaved abominably and deserved whatever punishment he decreed. She had never struck another person in her life — she had no idea what had possessed her to hit him. A lock of her hair fell annoyingly across her face and she raised her injured hand to push it back.

Before she could react he had taken it gently in his own and was examining it. 'Sweetheart, you little idiot, I think you have broken this. I should have realised the damage you did to my nose would have inflicted similar injury to your hand.'

A slight sound behind them made her jump. Her cousin was peering around the door. 'Is it safe to come in yet? Have you made peace or do you still wish to tear Charity limb from limb, your grace?'

He smiled and his eyes twinkled. 'I have decided to forgive Miss Lawson, but only because she also has sustained a serious injury. However, I have yet to deal with you, young lady.' He moved with such speed that her cousin was unable to retreat and found herself yanked unceremoniously into the sitting room and pushed onto the settle.

He proceeded to give her a set-down of such severity Patience was in floods of tears before he finished. Twice Charity had stepped forward to intervene but he had given her a warning shake of his head. So she hovered anxiously waiting for the tirade to end.

'I hope I make myself abundantly clear. You have had the most fortunate escape but this time your stupidity will not result in your ruin.' He stared sternly at her cousin. 'I am sorely tempted to put you across my knee and spank some sense into you.'

Patience didn't see the smile he directed at Charity and took him seriously. She shot to her feet and fled back into the bedchamber slamming the door and bolting it behind her.

Instead of taking him to task Charity returned his smile. 'That was well done, your grace, I doubt my uncle would have reduced her to tears. You can be very sure she will not do anything so silly again.'

'Living as she does in the wilds of the countryside it's hardly surprising she was taken in by the first attractive gentleman who paid her attention. I shall keep her on a tight rein throughout the Season and make sure she behaves herself.'

'That won't be necessary, sir, as we intend to return to Essex immediately. We cannot remain with Lady Harriet after this debacle — we have caused more upset this past week than she's had in her lifetime.'

An unexpected knock on the door startled her. What now? Then she relaxed as she recalled Mary was still missing. She was about to run and open it but he shook his head. 'You have a maid to do such tasks. Let her open the door.'

She smothered a giggle. 'No doubt she would be happy to oblige if she were not locked in the bedchamber with my cousin.' Ignoring his fulminating stare she walked to the door and opened it. To her delight not only was Mary standing there holding a laden tray but a second girl stood behind her equally burdened.

'Come in, we were wondering what was keeping you. Put the trays on the sideboard.'

When the second girl had gone Mary hovered by the bedchamber door giving the duke anxious glances. He shrugged and strolled to the exit. 'I shall leave you to your repast, sweetheart. I find that I am not at all hungry, you know. I wonder why that could be.' His rich, deep chuckle filled the room. The door was half-closed behind him when he spoke again. 'You will not be returning to Essex until the end of the Season. I have made other arrangements for you both.'

Before she could protest at his high-handed actions he was gone. She could hardly storm after him with the maid listening to every word. The girl would no doubt have noted his unnecessary endearment and drawn an erroneous conclusion. Botheration! He was making this so much more difficult for both of them. She was quite determined not to marry him and be the cause of them losing his estates, however painful that might be for both of them.

He had obligations to his name and his inheritance and if *he* could not see how unsuitable a match with her would be, then she was very sure that his acquaintances and family would soon explain it to him. She had no intention of being there when this happened. They would return to Essex whatever he might think.

The bedchamber door opened and her cousin rushed out. Her face was unusually pale and her eyes red and puffy, but there was something else that was different about her. Something intangible — she wasn't quite sure what it was. Then she realised her cousin seemed diminished, less confident, as though she had lost her *joie de vivre*.

'I hope you are as hungry as I am, Patience, because the kitchen has sent up even more than they did last time.'

'Mary asked for sufficient to feed all four of us. Shall we invite them to join us?'

'No, they must eat when we have finished. The duke might return and I have no wish to antagonise him further tonight.'

Her cousin snorted. 'I hardly think that's likely. He is besotted with you. He threatened to beat me and I wasn't the one who broke his nose and pushed him over!'

'He was jesting, Patience, I'm quite certain he would never raise his hand to either of us, however badly we behaved.'

'We didn't think that half an hour ago, cousin, otherwise we wouldn't have locked the door. If I recall correctly,' she continued smugly, 'he almost burst through the door in his rage. I am absolutely certain if he had gained entry then it would have been you put across his knee.'

A slight shiver trickled down Charity's spine. 'Nonsense, he might have raged and shouted but he wouldn't have laid a finger on me.' She sounded convinced of this but inside she wasn't sure. After all, she barely knew the man, had only met him a little over a week ago. The sooner they returned to the safety of the country the better.

There was little left on the trays by the time all of them had eaten. Mary and Sally took the trays to the kitchen themselves as they had yet to find a second truckle bed.

As soon as they had gone Charity broached the subject of returning home. 'I have no wish to remain in Town. We will be happy and safer in Essex with our families.'

'Surprisingly I agree with you, I have lost my taste for entertainment and society. However, if we do go back we will have to come up with a suitable reason as I have no wish to tell my parents any further falsehoods.'

'I had not thought of that. We were both so eager to go that I can think of no explanation for our sudden return, apart from the truth.'

'Mary told me that the duke said he had made alternative arrangements for us. He seems very determined that we remain. I can think of only one reason and that is that he is intending to pay court to you.'

'I told you before what we said to each other was a moment's aberration, no sensible person can imagine themselves in love after so short a space of time. It would be foolish of me indeed to say I don't find him very attractive, but that is no basis for a sound relationship. Also a duke in need of an heiress cannot marry a penniless vicar's daughter. Whatever our feelings on the matter, I am adamant I will not be instrumental in him losing his properties.'

She had expected her cousin to protest, but she shook her head sadly. 'I fear you are right. All this is my fault, if I had not insisted we exchange places he would not have allowed himself to fall in love with you. Now it is too late — what is done cannot be so easily undone.'

'That is fustian, and you know it, my love, for you were head over heels in love with Pettigrew yesterday and now you hold him in intense dislike.'

'You cannot compare the cases, Charity. Pettigrew proved himself to be a villain, my eyes were opened and I saw him as he truly was. The duke is a perfect match for you.' She clapped her hands. 'Would you marry him if you had a dowry?'

'I'm not sure, I have no wish to marry anybody at the present time, even someone as illustrious and handsome as him.'

Her cousin was not to be put off by her denial. 'I am quite sure that if you were in fact me, then you would marry him immediately. Your scruples are making you deny your true feelings.' She stood up, looking more like her old self, and nodded vigorously. 'We will not return ignominiously to the country, we will remain in London and enjoy the Season. By May I shall have found a solution to your problem and you will be able to accept his offer and become a duchess.'

* * *

Hugo had stolen their supper on impulse, not to punish either girl, but because he was hungry and the food would be cold by the time they emerged from the bedchamber. If she had paused to ask before she'd attacked him, he would have told her he had sent down for replacement trays and she would not be without her food.

He had plans to make if he was to obtain his objective and persuade Charity to accept his offer. He touched his nose and winced. She packed a punch that would do justice to a pugilist. When they were married he would have to do his best not to antagonise her. He had been furious for a minute or two and she was wise to have locked herself away from him. Would he have vented his anger in a physical way?

He closed his eyes and relived the moment. He could not remember having ever been so enraged with anyone or anything. He shuddered and a wave of shame engulfed him. He had a horrible feeling that if he had got his hands on her he might have done something unforgivable. This gave him pause for thought — he was not a violent man and had no wish to inflict physical harm on the woman he loved.

If being in each other's company engendered such violent emotions in them then he could possibly be endangering both of them by pursuing his quest. He was certain Charity would not have reacted with such violence to any other person but himself. Love was a strong emotion — perhaps they would both be better off seeking a partner where only affection and respect were involved in the relationship.

12

Overnight the snow melted and after breakfasting in their rooms Charity and her cousin were waiting for the summons to go downstairs and board the carriage.

'There's been a deal of toing and froing outside, Patience, but I have yet to see the duke or our carriage appear in the yard. I wonder if he's waiting for your luggage to arrive from the farm.'

Her cousin shrugged. She seemed remarkably subdued this morning and had eaten almost nothing. 'Possibly, but there will scarcely be space inside the carriage for the four of us and my luggage. Will we be going back to Lady Harriet, or somewhere else entirely?'

Charity's attention was attracted by a familiar figure striding across the cobbles. 'There he is. Shall I bang on the window?'

'God forbid! Haven't we done enough to disgust him?'

Reluctantly she joined her cousin by the fire. 'I don't like being ignored like an unwanted package. We need to know what is going on and where we will be taken when we do eventually leave here.'

'I have every confidence that his grace has the matter in hand. Do sit still, Charity, your fidgeting is making me dizzy.'

A further tedious half an hour dragged by before word was sent for them to go down. 'At last, it will be time for luncheon before we reach London, and we still don't know our direction. I do think the duke could have had the courtesy to speak to us himself this morning and explain what is going to happen. After all, he is supposed to be our guardian, isn't he?'

'Please don't say anything that will anger him, Charity, I find him quite terrifying when he is angry.'

Her cousin's words gave her pause. He was certainly a formidable man and not at all the sort of husband she had envisaged for herself. She had no wish for a volatile relationship, she preferred a quiet life with civilised conversation and companionship. If she were to marry the duke she would be forever anxious about offending him, and life would not be at all comfortable for either of them.

'I have come to a firm decision, Patience; after serious reflection I realise the duke and I are not at all suited. I believe he has come to the same conclusion which is why he hasn't spoken to me today. You do realise this means we cannot possibly remain under his control and have no option but to return to our respective homes immediately?'

'Very well, we shall go home. If I'm honest, I have had enough of London too. Perhaps we could tell our parents that we exchanged identities and that when we were discovered we were asked to leave. Although this is reprehensible, it is far better than the actual truth.'

There was no further opportunity for

chatter as they were in the crowded vestibule. The duke was waiting for them, he nodded and smiled politely, but things were definitely not the same between them.

'Good morning, your carriage awaits. Your luggage is now returned to you, Lady Patience, which is why there has been a slight delay this morning. I shall ride ahead and speak to you when we arrive.' He nodded a second time and strode off, not even waiting to escort them outside.

This time there were no hot bricks for her feet and insufficient rugs for all four of them. Her breath, as she spoke, clouded around her head. 'If we sit close together we can each share a blanket. Fortunately the journey is not long and we will soon be somewhere warm.'

They had been travelling for a quarter of an hour when she began to feel unwell. 'I fear I have caught a head cold, Patience. I feel distinctly feverish and my throat is raw.'

Her cousin reached out and touched her forehead. 'You are very hot, my love, you cannot possibly continue all the way to Essex as you are. You will go down with a putrid sore throat or develop congestion of the lungs if you do.'

'I cannot understand why I feel so wretched when I was perfectly well an hour ago. I insist that we go home, I doubt that my condition will worsen dramatically if I am obliged to spend a further few hours in the carriage.' Talking was difficult, her head felt as if it had been stuffed with wool and her throat as if she had swallowed broken glass.

When the carriage eventually pulled up she was in no condition to protest. She didn't have the energy to get out when footmen appeared to let down the steps. She would feel better if she had a little sleep right where she was.

★　★　★

Hugo pushed his mount to its limit in order to reach London ahead of the carriage and give himself time to organise the housing of his temporary wards. With luck his sister would already have arrived and take the girls in hand. He had no intention of remaining under the same roof as Charity, he would remove to his club and stay there until the end of the Season.

He clattered into his own stable yard, dismounted smoothly and tossed the reins to a waiting stableboy. 'The carriage will be here within the hour, make sure everything is ready to receive the team for they have had a wretched night of it.'

The house was delightfully warm after his uncomfortable ride. He paused in the entrance hall and smiled. The place was different — his sister must be in residence. He threw his riding coat to a waiting footman and tossed his hat and gloves and whip onto a side table.

His butler appeared before him. 'Good morning, your grace, Lady

Annabel is in the Green Room. She arrived first thing this morning.'

'Good, are the rooms prepared for my wards?' The man nodded. 'And the baby? How is he?'

The austere expression on his butler's face softened. 'Baby Richard is doing splendidly, your grace. He is a firm favourite with all your staff.' The man realised he had spoken out of turn and for the first time in their long acquaintance Mullins looked uncomfortable.

'I'm glad to hear it, I shall be up to see for myself as soon as I've spoken to Lady Annabel. Send word to the kitchen that a hot luncheon will be required as soon as the young ladies arrive.'

There was no need to bother about changing his soiled raiment just to speak to his sister — they stood on no ceremony. He strode through the house, not surprised she had chosen this chamber as it was smaller and warmer than the grand drawing room.

He pushed open the door and was

greeted by a shriek of pleasure. 'Hugo, there you are at last. Do you have the runaway safely back?'

'I do indeed, her reputation is intact. I am delighted to see you, my dear Annabel, and looking so radiant too. Married life is obviously still to your taste — how is Radley? He did not object to me stealing you for the Season?'

His sister pursed her lips. 'Surely you do not think we are to be separated for so long? He is to join us at the end of the week and will remain here as long as I do.' She laughed and shook her head. 'No, brother, do not look so anguished. I promise you will not be obliged to spend time alone with him.'

'I think your husband is a splendid fellow, I did not hesitate to give my permission when he asked for your hand two years ago — however, his preoccupation with things astrological bores me to tears. Anyway, I intend to move to my club. I have decided that even with you staying here, it might be best not to give the gossips anything to discuss.'

'Don't be ridiculous, Hugo, are you so desperate to avoid being leg-shackled that you are obliged to hide from an eligible heiress?'

He ignored her question and began to tell her about the rescued baby. 'I am at a loss to understand why his disappearance has not been announced somewhere. He obviously comes from a good home and I cannot believe his parents are not beside themselves with worry.'

'He must come from the country. You must widen your search — send people to make enquiries much further afield. I cannot wait to meet the little fellow. I am hopeful that maybe next year I might present you with a nephew or niece.'

Annabel had lost a baby in the early stages of pregnancy last autumn and had been advised to avoid a second pregnancy for at least a year. 'I'm sure that you will, my dear, but until that time enjoy the parties and balls that are on offer. I have to send a note to Aunt Harry, and then we shall go up and you can meet him yourself.'

They were returning from a satisfactory visit to the nursery when two footmen hurried across the hallway and opened the front door. The carriage was here. He wasn't sure either young lady would be particularly pleased to find themselves under his roof when they expected to return to their own homes in Essex.

His sister would be presenting them and he would escort them to a few parties, just enough to make sure they were well-established in society, and then keep his distance. Of course, he would make sure Lady Patience was not importuned by fortune hunters again, and that they got into no further scrapes, but that was all. If he spent any time alone with Charity he would be unable to suppress his feelings and a union between the two of them would not do.

He was about to turn away and wait with his sister when Lady Patience flew in through the door. 'Your grace, come at once, Charity has been taken ill and cannot get out of the carriage.'

'Tell my sister, she is in the Green Room,' he called as he pounded down the steps and out to the carriage. Charity was slumped in one corner with the two maids attempting to lift her from the seat without success.

'Let me carry her.' Immediately they shuffled to the far side of the carriage, making it rock alarmingly. He reached in and slid one hand under her knees and the other around her shoulders. 'Sweetheart, it is I, you will be well now, I'm here to take care of you.'

Fortunately his arms were long enough to allow him to pick her up without climbing in himself. After carefully stepping away from the carriage he turned and almost ran across the pavement and back into the house. His sister was already in the vestibule.

'Let me look at her, Hugo, I can

decide if she needs the attention of the physician.' Annabel felt for a pulse somewhere under Charity's ear and then brushed her fingers across her forehead. 'Her temperature is alarmingly high. I shall send someone for the doctor right away. Hugo, it would be better if she had a chamber away from anyone else until we are sure what it is she has gone down with.'

'Burson has put the girls together — however, I'm certain Lady Patience can sleep elsewhere for the moment. God knows, this house is big enough to sleep a dozen visitors.'

'Was Miss Lawson unwell yesterday?'

Her cousin answered from behind them. 'She was perfectly fine until an hour ago. We were talking and then she said her throat hurt and before a quarter of an hour had passed she was almost delirious with fever and unable to stand.'

He had reached the apartment intended for both girls and shouldered his way in. Patience dodged past him and into the bedchamber and pulled back the covers. 'There is little point in my being kept from my cousin, or for Mary and Sally, we have been closeted together in the confines of the carriage for the past hour and a half. If whatever Charity has contracted is infectious, then we have already caught it.'

Annabel answered, 'I fear you are right. Hugo, put Miss Lawson down and come away at once. We must leave the nursing to those who have been in close contact with her. You must ensure whatever illness it is does not reach the nursery floor. Therefore, neither of us must visit the baby again for the moment.'

He wasn't used to being given instructions by young ladies, but both of them were correct. He would postpone his decision to move out until he was sure Charity would recover and that no one else succumbed to this mystery illness.

'If you will excuse me, Annabel, I will change my garments and then return to the Green Room. There are several things we need to discuss.'

*　*　*

Charity awoke in a strange chamber and for a moment was confused. Then she recalled that she'd been taken unwell in the coach. She needed the commode most urgently. She pushed herself up on her elbows and was shocked at how weak and dizzy she was.

'Miss Lawson, you must not attempt to get out of bed on your own. You have been very poorly these past three days.' The speaker was someone she vaguely recognised, but could not remember her name.

'Where is my abigail? She can assist me to the commode.'

'I'm afraid that Lady Patience, Sally and Mary all succumbed to the same thing that has been afflicting you. I am the housekeeper here, Mrs Burson, I have been taking care of you.'

The short walk to the screen, behind

which the necessary item was hidden, exhausted her and she was relieved to be helped back into bed. 'How long have I been unwell? Is my cousin also recovering?'

'You arrived here three days ago. Lady Patience is still very poorly, but the doctor is confident she will make a full recovery in time.'

'I hope that no one else in this establishment has caught my unpleasant illness. Have the duke and baby Richard remained fit?'

'Yes, miss, we have all been careful to stay away from the nursery. I sent for some broth and lemonade as soon as I saw you waking. You will feel a deal better when you have taken something to eat and drink.'

Charity managed most of the lemonade but only a few mouthfuls of the broth before her eyes closed and she drifted off to sleep again. Two days passed in a similar manner before she was feeling well enough to take an interest in her surroundings.

She insisted on getting up and taking a bath. Her hand was an interesting shade of blue and yellow but appeared not to be broken. The warm water helped with her aching limbs and she stepped out ready to get dressed and determined to visit the other invalids.

The girl who was taking care of her seemed reluctant to talk and Charity had not the energy to insist. With her hair arranged in an attractive knot on top of her head, and wearing a long-sleeved gown in pink sprigged muslin, she was ready to venture out of her apartment and visit her cousin.

'Please direct me to Lady Patience.'

The girl curtsied and mumbled something unintelligible, and scurried across, opened the sitting room door and pointed down the spacious passageway. There were three similar doors — which one contained Patience? She turned to ask but the girl had vanished.

Her legs were still a trifle wobbly, but if she moved slowly and stayed within arm's reach of the wall, she believed she could negotiate the short distance safely. She was halfway to the first of the doors when she heard heavy footsteps approaching.

'Good grief! What are you doing out here? You should be resting in your chamber not traipsing about in the corridor on your own.' The duke arrived beside her and without a by your leave snatched her from the ground and strode back the way she'd come.

'Please, your grace, I need to see Patience. Something is wrong, I'm sure of it, and until I've seen my cousin I shall fear the worst.'

He swore under his breath. 'No one has told you? I promise you your cousin is on the mend.' He said no more but kicked her sitting room door open and marched in. He gently put her down on a *chaise longue* placed conveniently by the roaring applewood fire. To her astonishment he sat next to her and took her hands gently in his. 'Sweetheart, I'm most dreadfully sorry to tell you, but your abigail, Sally, passed away yesterday. Mary is fighting for her life but the doctor fears there will not be a happy outcome in her case either.'

For a second she could not take it in. 'Sally is dead and Mary could die also?' He nodded solemnly and squeezed her hands in sympathy. 'I killed them, they are dead because of me.'

'That's balderdash, my dear girl, and well you know it. I've made enquiries at the inn and it seems that a dozen or more guests went down with the same illness. I was there, but I have escaped the infection. You are no more to blame than the wind or the snow.'

'I've only known the girls since we left home — but I am still grieved at Sally's death and pray that Mary might somehow recover.'

'You don't look at all well, you should not be out of bed, I gave strict instructions that you remain there for at least another three days.'

She managed a weak smile. 'Your grace, I am sure we should not be discussing such a matter. I am up now, and whatever you say, as soon as you go, I shall make my way to my cousin.'

He was still holding her hands and she was enjoying the comfort and strength they gave her. 'You will do no such thing. In fact, I shall remain here with you to ensure that you do as I bid.'

'In which case, your grace — '

'Enough of this 'your grace' nonsense. My name is Hugo, I insist in future that you address me by my given name. I shall call you Charity.'

She snatched her hands back, shocked to the core by his outrageous suggestion. 'We cannot, we must not, I am a vicar's daughter . . . '

He interrupted her a second time. 'What the hell does that have to do with anything? I am a duke and if I wish us to address each other informally, then that is what will happen and nobody will have the temerity to mention the matter.'

'I don't care what you say, your grace, I have behaved appallingly these past days and have no intention of compounding my sins and doing as you suggest.' She tried to look cross, but her vision had become unpleasantly blurry.

From a distance she heard further ungentlemanly language and then heard nothing at all.

13

A further few days drifted past before Charity was finally recovered from her illness. She was relieved to hear that Mary was also on the mend and her cousin eager to receive visitors. After her ablutions she wandered into the closet to find it full to bursting with new gowns, plus all the underpinnings, bonnets and bits and pieces necessary to make a perfect ensemble.

She had yet to learn the name of her new maid. 'When did these arrive? I can't believe the seamstress and her girls have completed my new wardrobe so promptly.'

'They came yesterday, Miss Lawson, ever so pretty they are. I reckon you can wear a different gown every day for a month.'

'I shall leave you to select something suitable. What is your name? We cannot deal well together until I know that.'

The girl curtsied. 'I'm Maisie, miss, and his grace says as I am to look after you whilst you're here.'

'Well, I'm pleased to meet you. I have no intention of venturing outside today so a morning gown will be suitable.'

She barely glanced at herself in the glass but was assured several times that the leaf-green Indian cotton suited her perfectly.

'Your breakfast tray is waiting in your sitting room, miss, there's ever so much on it. I reckon Cook has been told to send up a bit of everything she has to tempt your appetite.'

As Charity opened the communicating door she was greeted by a delicious aroma of hothouse flowers. She stared around in amazement at the array of vases and baskets of exotic fruit that covered every surface.

'Good heavens! I'd no idea the duke had a hothouse here.' She ignored the tray and instead selected something from the fruit basket.

'He don't, miss, he sent out for all these.'

Her appetite deserted her. The duke — or Hugo, as he wished her to call him — could not afford to waste his money on such fripperies. Were these gifts a sign that he intended to continue his pursuit or had he done the same for her cousin? Whatever the reason he must not spend any further funds on her or Patience.

'I'm going to see my cousin. Which door do I need?'

'The second one on the right, Miss Lawson.' The girl looked agitated and was wringing her hands in her apron.

'What is wrong?'

'I was told I must make sure you eat your breakfast. I'll be in for it if I take this tray back untouched.'

'Why don't you eat it yourself? I'm sure you must be hungry — Sally always was.'

'I daren't, I'm no good at telling lies, miss, and I'd be found out immediately.'

'I don't wish you to get into trouble on my behalf so I'll eat enough to keep Cook happy.'

In fact, when she bit into a slice of bread with butter and marmalade she discovered she was hungry. A full half an hour later she put down her cutlery, drained a bowl of chocolate, wiped her mouth on the napkin and stood up. 'I am replete, please tell Cook my breakfast was quite delicious.'

The skirt of her new gown was crumb-covered and she hastily shook them off. 'Thank you for insisting I broke my fast, Maisie, I feel so much better for having eaten. If anyone should enquire, I am with Lady Patience.'

She recalled her first attempt to reach her cousin and checked the corridor was empty before venturing from her sitting room. She had no intention of being manhandled a second time. She knocked and heard footsteps approaching. The door opened and a maid bobbed politely.

'Please to come in, Miss Lawson, her

ladyship is expecting you.'

Charity was scarcely inside the sitting room when a well-remembered voice called from the bedchamber. 'At last, I have so much to tell you. Charity, you must come in here at once.'

Her mouth curved. Her cousin had obviously recovered her spirits. She hurried into a bedchamber that was identical in every way to the one she was using — this too had faded hangings and threadbare carpet. Patience was propped up in bed in a froth of lacy pillows. She ran across and embraced her.

'I am so glad to see you looking so well. Indeed, I think you have more colour than I do. I'm surprised you are not up and in your sitting room.'

'Mama insists I remain in bed until she gives me leave to move.'

'Aunt Faith is here? I can't believe she has left your siblings and come to Town.'

'I know, I believe the duke's sister sent for her. He also sent for your parents but the little ones have the chickenpox and your mama could not leave them. I'm sure she has sent you a letter — did you not see one in your sitting room?'

'I didn't look, I shall investigate when I return. We have caused so much upheaval and expense to this household, Patience. The sooner we return to Essex the better.' She gestured to her new gown. 'Have you had the energy to look in your closet? I've more clothes than I shall wear in a year. No doubt fashions will have changed long before I get to wear them all.'

'Fiddlesticks to that! Now we are well we are to attend a soirée somewhere very prestigious and be introduced to society. I'm hoping that Lady Annabel Radley, the duke's sister, will present us and that Papa will foot the bill. His grace will not be out of pocket — indeed, you will benefit from us staying here as all his household bills will be paid.'

Her cousin seemed so animated, and had already forgotten her unpleasant experience. Charity had no wish to spoil her fun, but had no intention of remaining in Town herself especially if her mother was coping with poorly children on her own. She was about to explain this then thought better of it. 'How exciting! Have you managed to keep your little adventure secret from your mama?'

'The subject has not arisen. You can be very sure the staff here will not divulge anything — they would lose their positions if they did. I don't wish to talk about it anymore; it is in the past and quite forgotten.' She clapped her hands and gave her a knowing look. 'I believe that you will make a match of it with the duke. Mama is quite put out that he has settled on you, a vicar's daughter with no dowry, and not chosen me instead.'

'I shall not marry him even if he did offer for me, which he has not and will not. We have discussed this matter and decided we do not suit and that he must do the right thing and marry an heiress.' She swallowed a lump in her throat as she spoke. The thought of him belonging to another quite broke her heart.

Patience stared at her as if she was an escapee from Bedlam. 'I cannot believe what I'm hearing. Have you run mad? Not marry a duke? If he offered for me I should accept with alacrity even though my feelings are not engaged. He must be the handsomest man in London. The fact that he has debts and is short of funds would be no obstacle to me.'

Charity wanted to stamp her foot. 'Of course it wouldn't be, you goose, *you* are an heiress. If he married me he would lose his estates and have nothing but debts to pass on to his heirs. Even if my feelings were engaged, which I can assure you they are not, I could not let him ruin his life in that way.' Her cousin was about to continue the debate but she had no wish to discuss it further.

'I am going downstairs to introduce

myself to Lady Annabel. Will you be getting up today?'

'I shall do so when Mama returns — I can't imagine why she's been gone so long. Perhaps she is in the nursery, you know how she is with babies.'

'Indeed I do. In fact I shall go to there first as I haven't seen baby Richard since he arrived here. The duke has obviously not discovered his parents. The poor little thing will have forgotten them if he is here much longer.'

She left her cousin reading a magazine and went to her own apartment in order to get directions to the nursery. The passageways and corridors were icy so she must find a spencer or a shawl before she ventured elsewhere. Maisie must have gone to have her breakfast as her apartment was empty. Charity quickly found a pretty cashmere shawl which complemented her outfit perfectly.

The nursery must be on the floor above, so all she had to do was find a flight of stairs leading upwards and no doubt she would discover the rooms she wanted. She walked back to the gallery and sure enough there was a less imposing staircase which must take her to the nursery floor.

It was equally chilly up here, she hoped the actual nursery was warmer than the corridor outside. There were several doors on either side of the passageway; this was flooded with weak sunlight from a large window at the far end. She picked a door at random and walked in.

The room was the schoolroom, the furniture shrouded in holland sheets and everything dusty and neglected. She deduced if the schoolrooms were on the left side of the passage then the bedrooms should be on the right. She emerged and selected the door across the way.

As soon as she pushed it open she knew her choice was correct. The room was blissfully warm, a cheerful fire burning at a grate at either end. This was the playroom and Richard was sitting on a blanket happily playing with a pile of bricks.

Two adoring nursemaids were there to take care of him — one on her knees on the carpet encouraging him to knock down the towers she was building. The girls jumped to their feet and curtsied and Richard crowed with delight and held out his arms. How could he possibly recognise her as his saviour after so long apart?

'Good morning, darling baby, I've come to see how you are doing.'

She bent down and scooped him up and he patted her face and babbled nonsense at her.

One of the nursemaids exclaimed in surprise. 'Look at that, Mary, I've never seen the like. He's not done more than smile for any of his other visitors, apart from his grace, of course.'

Charity carried the baby over to a rocking chair, being careful not to knock her injured hand, and sat down with him on her lap. 'Well, little one, I can see that you're happy and well. I'm sorry I could not visit you before but your Aunt Charity has been very poorly.'

She rocked him to and fro and the baby clapped his hands and chuckled, but unexpectedly he put his thumb in his mouth, closed his eyes and fell asleep in her arms. She stroked his head, loving the feel of his soft hair beneath her fingers. The weight of his body against her breasts felt right. His parents must be distraught; if anyone stole her baby she would happily shoot them dead herself.

Shocked by her thoughts she stiffened and the baby wriggled in protest. 'It's all right, sweetheart, you sleep for a while, I have nothing better to do.'

The two girls were hovering a few yards away. 'If you have other duties to perform, you may go and do them. Richard will be fine with me. If I have need of anyone I will ring.'

The girls didn't protest, they curtsied again and whisked away through a door to the left of the fireplace at the far end.

She continued to rock gently back and forth and carefully pulled the end of her shawl around the sleeping infant. Her eyes flickered shut and she relaxed, it would do no harm for her to doze for a while — the visit downstairs to meet Lady Annabel could wait until this afternoon.

* * *

Hugo stared around the empty sitting room and frowned. He had expected to find Charity sitting quietly in here reading a book — where the devil was she? He shouted for attention but no girl came in from the bedchamber to attend to him.

She must be with her cousin but he could hardly barge in there unannounced. Although he'd decided last week that it would be folly to continue his pursuit, her illness and near demise had shown him that he couldn't live without her. They would live in Northumbria and no doubt fight like cat and dog, but they would be happy. He realised that without her at his side his life would be meaningless — what use were riches and estates if you were miserable?

He knocked politely on the door and a few moments later it was opened by a nervous maid. 'Is Miss Lawson within?'

'No, your grace, she left a while ago.'

Charity wasn't downstairs or he would have seen her, so the only other place she could be was in the nursery visiting Richard. The baby had only been in his charge for two weeks but already he felt like part of the family and it was going to be a dreadful wrench when eventually they found his parents and had to hand him over. He bounded up the nursery stairs, but pushed open the playroom door slowly so as not to startle the baby.

He stopped, his breath caught in his throat and his eyes filled. He had never seen anything so beautiful as the girl he loved to distraction asleep with the baby in her arms. He stepped in and quietly closed the door behind him, he didn't want to wake either of them. Richard had never looked so content, as if he belonged where he was, and Hugo noticed for the first time that the baby had similar colouring to Charity. Corn-coloured hair and sparkling blue eyes — she could be his mother.

Their child might well look like this infant — maybe next year he would have a son or daughter of his own. He carefully carried an armchair over and placed it next to them. He wanted to watch them sleep and think about how he could persuade his darling girl that living anywhere but at his side was an impossibility.

He stretched out his booted foot and began to rock the chair; it would do both of them good to rest awhile. He studied her face more closely and was shocked to see how thin and pale she had become since her illness. Perhaps he had better bide his time until she was fully recovered. Although she had expressed a desire to return to Essex she could not possibly do so whilst her siblings were suffering from the chickenpox.

The countess had assured him that it would not be safe for Charity to be at the vicarage until all four children had recovered as she had not contracted the disease when she was young. However, Patience would leave with her mama the next day. The poor girl was as yet unaware she was to be removed from London. He was almost sure Lady Faith was aware of the unfortunate escapade and this was why she was determined to take her wayward daughter home. Nothing had been said, but servants talked and something must have filtered through to her.

The fires crackled and his beloved continued to doze. He looked up as a nursery maid peeped around the door, he smiled and shook his head and they were alone again.

'Your grace, I do beg your pardon, have you been here long?'

He sat up abruptly, forgetting his foot

was on the rocker of the chair and almost ejected the two occupants. She was only able to remain seated by clutching the arm, which woke the baby, and he screamed his protest.

'Devil take it! I apologise for waking Richard — '

She smiled and he was almost unmanned. 'And for attempting to tip us on the floor?' She gently stroked the baby and he settled down again. A nursemaid slipped in and removed the sleeping infant, no doubt taking him to his crib where he could sleep in comfort and peace.

'Of course, sweetheart, I would do nothing to hurt either of you.' He had her full attention now. 'I know I can be bad-tempered and brusque, but I give you my word as a gentleman I would never do more than shout at you.'

Her gurgle of laughter did something strange to his insides. 'Well, sir, that is indeed a comfort to me. There's nothing I enjoy more than being shouted at by a large and formidable gentleman.'

By force of will he remained in his seat and did not reach over and snatch her into his arms. 'If you refer to me again by anything other than my given name I shall take umbrage.' He scowled at her but she was not fooled for a moment.

'I told you before, I have broken enough rules already and have no wish to compound my sins by addressing you so informally. I understand from my aunt that even married couples refer to each other by their titles.'

'Can I persuade you to make a compromise? When we are alone, as we are now, would you please call me Hugo?'

14

How could she resist him when he asked her so sweetly? 'Very well, Hugo, as long as you understand that alone means that there are not even servants in attendance.'

Something flashed across his face that could have been triumph, but maybe she was mistaken. Having got his way, he changed the subject. 'I take it that you know you cannot return to Essex for a few weeks?'

'I do, Patience told me. She seems to be under the impression that we are to stay here for the Season as planned. Is that the case?'

He shook his head. 'Lady Faith is taking her home tomorrow, but I advise you not to say anything. Your cousin is unaware of the true circumstances — I fear her misdemeanours have not remained a secret from her parents.'

'How awful! But at least she came out of it with her reputation intact, thanks to you. When she has time to think about it she will understand she does not deserve to gallivant all over Town as if nothing has happened.' An unpleasant thought struck her. 'I sincerely hope I will not be expected to attend parties? I only agreed to come because my cousin couldn't come by herself.'

'I don't believe there is another young lady in the realm who would consider a ball or a soirée a punishment rather than a pleasure.' He stood up and before she could react grabbed her hands and yanked her from her seat. 'You have a wardrobe full of new gowns, I have pried my sister from the wilds of Hertfordshire to be your chaperone, I'm damned if I'm going to let you mope away indoors.'

'I thought you were appalled by such events?' He grinned and moved a little closer. 'I shall only go if you come with me. I refuse to suffer overcrowded, stuffy rooms and indifferent refreshments on my own.'

He was too close. His heat and masculinity all but overwhelmed her but she could not force her feet to move her out of danger. Then it was too late and his arms were around her and her softness was pressed against his chest. She intended to put her hands between them and push him away but they travelled of their own volition upwards until they were linked around his neck.

'Look at me, my darling, I wish to drown in your blue eyes.'

His ridiculous remark brought her to her senses and she stamped on his toe. As she was wearing her indoor slippers and he his boots this was no more than a gesture, but it had the desired effect. His arms dropped and she was free. For some unaccountable reason she did not immediately remove herself from his reach.

'You must not take liberties, sir, I will not be bamboozled into accepting your offer.'

He remained relaxed, no more than a foot away from her. 'I was not aware, Miss Lawson, that I had made you a second offer.' He grinned in a most disarming way. Before she could react he dropped to one knee in a dramatic fashion.

'My darling Charity, I insist that you make me the happiest of men and become my wife.' He sprang upright and seized her hands in a grip from which she could not release them. 'After all, as you so kindly pointed out, I have taken un-gentlemanly liberties and you have no option but to accept me.'

'I don't wish to marry you — we do not suit. And anyway you would never have offered for me in the first place if you had known my true identity. In fact, if I had not changed places with my cousin you would not have given me a second look.'

He raised an eyebrow but refused to release her. 'Did you behave differently because you had assumed your cousin's persona?'

'Of course I didn't.'

He nodded and his mouth curved into what could only be described as a smug smile. 'And neither did I, sweetheart. I would still have followed you to Green Park that first morning and we would still have found Richard.'

'But you must admit we were only invited so that you could pursue Patience and thus solve your financial difficulties.' She warmed to her theme. 'Don't you see, Hugo, you must marry an heiress. You cannot throw away your estates on something so whimsical as love.'

'If you don't marry me, sweetheart, I shall remain a bachelor and my title will die with me — do you wish to have that on your conscience?'

She tugged a little harder but her hands remained clasped firmly within his. 'I don't believe you. A handsome gentleman like yourself would never deny himself the comfort of a wife.'

His eyes glinted wickedly. 'I take it by your reference to comfort, you are referring to making love? I shall keep a string of ladybirds and deny myself nothing apart from a son to carry on the title.'

Her cheeks flushed; indeed, heat spread from her toes to the crown of her head. How could he mention such a thing to her? She had never been so embarrassed in her life. Then righteous indignation flooded her. He was toying with her, being deliberately provocative in order to elicit a response.

Instead of kicking him hard on the shins which no doubt was what he expected, she flung her arms around his neck and pressed herself close so that every inch of her was touching him. 'How clever of you to come up with a solution. You may offer me a *carte-blanche* and I shall accept. I will be your mistress and there will be no need for you to marry me.'

Her hands were free and he was staring at her in bemusement. She smiled sweetly. 'The fact that your children will be bastards is unfortunate, but I believe it is possible to get an Act of Parliament to legitimise a son born the wrong side of the blanket.' His expression changed to something far more dangerous.

'I am tempted to accept your offer, my love, but far more inclined to turn you over my knee instead.'

There was no time to escape, she would get her comeuppance and this would be no more than she deserved. She straightened and stared at him calmly, pleased she was able to hide her fear. 'I beg your pardon, your grace, for speaking so outrageously. However, I believe I have made my point. We seem to urge each other into unacceptable behaviour and this is no basis for a companionable marriage. I should like to go to my apartment, all this excitement has made me feel rather unwell.'

Instead of stepping aside he reached out and picked her up as if she weighed no more than a bag of feathers. 'In which case, darling, I shall take you back to your chamber immediately.'

It would be foolish to struggle and if she was honest, she wished to enjoy the comfort of his arms for the last time. She rested her head on his shoulder and allowed him to carry her down two flights of stairs. He gently placed her on her feet outside the door and bent his head to whisper in her ear.

'The last thing I want, sweetheart, is a *companionable* marriage. I want to wake up every morning with your lovely head beside me on the pillow and know that each day will be exciting.'

Before she could answer he reached around her, opened the door, and pushed her firmly through it. He closed it with a decided click behind her. She leant against the door and tried to organise her thoughts. He was so determined to marry her that her resolve was weakening. Would she not be considered foolish to refuse to marry a duke however impecunious he might be?

She flopped down on the nearest chair, bewildered by his insistence. As there were dozens of young ladies more beautiful than her, and hundreds who were from better families and had a dowry, she could only suppose that love had blinded him to her imperfections.

Her heart skipped a beat whenever she saw him and her toes curled in their slippers when he smiled at her — did this mean she was in love with him? She might be a naive country miss but she recognised an attractive gentleman when she saw one. No, she needed a sterner test than that. How would she feel if he were to marry another?

She would be jealous and miserable, but did this prove she was in love with him? What if he were to contract a fatal illness — how would she feel then? She clutched her chest and tears spilled from her eyes. If anything were to happen to him her own life would be over.

She jumped to her feet knowing she had answered her own questions. She loved him and would marry him regardless of the consequences. She would find him at once and tell him the good news. The passageway outside was empty and she raced in a most unladylike manner to the gallery and peered over the balustrade. There he was, and he had his coat on so must be going out.

Without stopping to think how he might react she yelled down. 'Your grace, I must speak with you.' Her voice echoed dramatically increasing the volume to a deafening level. His reaction was all she could have hoped for. His feet left the ground and he dropped his whip and gloves on the floor.

Not waiting for him to answer, she gathered up her skirts in one hand and grabbed the banister in the other and ran down the stairs. She arrived in front of him in a swirl of petticoats and exposed ankles.

'Can we go somewhere private to speak? I have something most urgent to tell you.'

He stared down at her from his prodigious height, his lips were tight and his expression not particularly welcoming. 'Are you sure you would not like to shout your news to me like a fishwife?'

Only then was she aware of the butler standing to attention and trying not to snigger. Too late to repine — the damage was done. 'It is unpleasantly cold standing here, your grace. I do not have the benefit of a heavy coat to keep me warm. I would much prefer to continue our conversation somewhere warm.' She tossed her head and despite his frosty glare she couldn't prevent her smile. Was she turning into her cousin? She had never tossed her head in her life before.

She was about to head for the drawing room when he restrained her with a hand on her elbow. 'My sister is in there, we can go into an anteroom.' He guided her towards a door and all but bundled her into the icy chamber. 'Be quick, Charity, I'm on my way out and don't wish to keep my horses standing.'

She was tempted to keep her exciting news to herself as he was being so curmudgeonly. 'Hugo, I came especially to tell you that I love you and accept your kind offer and wish to be your wife.'

She expected him to snatch her up and kiss her, spin her around in delight now that he had won the hand of the young lady he was supposedly in love with. Instead he sighed heavily and continued to frown at her. 'I am not sure that I wish to marry anyone who thinks it acceptable to shriek at me the way you just did. Whatever my financial status, I am the Duke of Edbury and have a position to maintain.'

Her happiness evaporated like snow in the sunshine. 'I thought you loved me?'

Then he roared with laughter and she was enveloped in a hug that almost crushed her ribs. 'Of course I love you, and I am ecstatic that you have finally realised you return my feelings. I was merely teaching you a lesson. My darling girl, you must refrain from your wild behaviour if you wish to be accepted in the best drawing rooms.'

She tipped her head back and grinned at him. 'As I have no wish to be accepted anywhere apart from your drawing room, I shall continue to do as I please.'

His answer was exactly what she wanted. His mouth covered hers and she lost herself in a few minutes of bliss. He eventually put her down. 'I would like to get married immediately.'

'Immediately? You cannot possibly do that — you must speak to my father. I have no intention of being married anywhere but in my own church and by my own father.'

He kissed the top of her head and brought her hands up to rest on his shirt front. 'I know, I was speaking from the heart, my love. I would love to marry you tomorrow but understand we must wait and do things correctly.'

'We have known each other such a short time, Hugo, I would like to get to know you better before we are wed. A June wedding would be perfect and that is only four months away.'

'Then June it will be. I must go, the carriage has been outside long enough. My sister is no doubt eager for news, so you must introduce yourself and tell her that we are to be married in the summer.'

He dropped a kiss, hard, on her open mouth and strode off. If she was not mistaken he was singing to himself. The drawing room doors were closed, but unlike Lady Harriet's residence there were no eager footmen waiting to fling them open and announce her.

Should she knock or was it acceptable to walk straight in? She decided on a compromise and knocked and opened the door simultaneously. There were now fires lit in this spacious chamber and she thought this was in honour of his sister who had tossed aside her book and jumped to her feet as Charity entered.

'Miss Lawson, I'm so glad to see you

up and about at last. My brother has been beside himself with worry these past few days. I am Annabel, in case you're wondering who the strange woman is sitting in the drawing room.'

His sister was above medium height, plump and had nut-brown curls. Only her eyes were similar to his, being an unusual shade of almost black.

Charity curtsied. 'I am delighted to make your acquaintance, Lady Annabel. Would you mind if I joined you?'

'I should be offended if you didn't, my dear. Come and sit down by the fire. You are even lovelier than I expected. Small wonder my brother is besotted.'

There was a vacant chair the opposite side of the fire and Charity took it. 'He said to tell you that we are getting married in June.' Saying the words out loud made the fact that she was engaged to be married to a duke seem even more unlikely. 'I know he should marry an heiress but he is adamant he will have nobody else but me. He told me that if I refuse to marry him the title would go in abeyance and that would be on my conscience.'

Lady Annabel laughed. 'How typical of him! I'm sure they would dig up a distant male relative from somewhere if needs be. My dear girl, am I to understand that you are reluctant to become a duchess?'

'I would much prefer not to, but as the man I love happens to be a duke, I have little option. Do you mind if I ask you exactly how dire his circumstances are?'

'He will have to sell this house and the main estate to cover the debts our father left him. However, he has several smaller estates in the North and these should bring in sufficient income to live comfortably, if not luxuriously.'

'I am used to living simply. It will be difficult moving so far away from my family but no doubt I shall survive the separation. Do you live near London, my lady?'

'Hertfordshire — my husband is

addicted to science but fortunately he has pockets deep enough to fund this hobby as well as keep me in funds and new gowns.'

They chatted companionably until the housekeeper came in to announce that a cold collation had been set out in the breakfast room. 'Lady Patience and the countess are on their way down to join you, Lady Annabel.'

Charity smiled at her. 'Have you met my cousin and my aunt? Patience and I are similar in looks but quite different in character.'

'I have met your aunt, my dear, and found her entertaining company. Unfortunately your cousin succumbed to the illness that laid you so low before I had the opportunity to meet her.'

The duke, presumably, was not returning for the midday repast. Most gentlemen devoured a substantial breakfast and then made do until dinner. 'What time do we dine here? Today will be the first time I have been well enough to come down.'

'As we will be family only, we shall

keep country hours. Dinner will be served at five o'clock.'

The passageway that led to the breakfast room was accessed from a door at the far end of the chamber and did not require them to walk through the freezing vestibule. Aunt Faith and Patience were ahead of them and they entered the room together. Her aunt introduced her cousin to Lady Annabel and then they took their seats around the table. A parlourmaid and a footman served soup and placed plates of cold cuts, chutneys, sweet rolls and butter in the centre of the table. Once this was done they disappeared discreetly.

'I'm glad to see you downstairs, Patience. Perhaps, now you are well we can go for a walk.'

Her aunt interrupted her. 'You shall do no such thing. We are returning home tomorrow morning and until then Patience will remain in the house. I have yet to decide if she is allowed to come down for dinner tonight.'

Her cousin hung her head and

Charity knew there was no point in arguing. Her aunt was naturally an indolent woman, but when she made up her mind there was no changing it. 'I shall be sorry to see you go, Aunt Faith, but understand the reasons for it. I should return with you if I could.'

Lady Annabel shook her head. 'Even if your siblings were not sick I should not allow you to leave. You have come for the Season and I have every intention of introducing my future sister-in-law to all the best families.'

15

This announcement caused Aunt Faith and Patience to gape at Charity as if she had grown two heads. Lady Annabel was unabashed by the reaction. 'I take it that neither of you were aware of this exciting news. It cannot become official until my brother has spoken to Mr Lawson but he is taking care of that right now.'

So that was where Hugo was off to in such a hurry earlier. He was obviously very sure of her feelings and had intended to ask permission to marry her before she had actually agreed. 'It must be somewhat of a shock to hear that I have become engaged to the duke after such a short acquaintance.'

Her aunt recovered her composure. 'My dear girl, you did the right thing. For a young lady in your position it would be foolhardy not to accept an offer from a duke, even if he was a complete stranger. Indeed, you are fortunate your duke is not in his dotage.'

Charity stared at her aunt in disbelief. 'I am marrying him because I love him and for no other reason. He should be marrying an heiress to restore his fortunes, but is prepared to forego such matters because he loves me too.'

'Am I to understand, Charity, that the Duke of Edbury is in financial difficulties?' Charity nodded. 'Then I am at a loss to see how this betrothal has come about. For you, my dear, even a duke with no money must be more than you can ever have dreamt of for a partner — but for him to contract an arrangement with a penniless girl beggars belief.'

Lady Annabel stepped in to smooth the situation. 'They are in love, Lady Faith, and as we know, 'love conquers all'. Once my brother made up his mind on the subject nothing will deflect him until he has achieved his aim. He will marry your niece or marry no one. Therefore, dear Charity is saving our name from extinction by agreeing to marry him and live in penury.'

'I think you are exaggerating a trifle, my lady. Although this house and the main estates in Surrey will be sold to pay the debts the Northern properties will remain. I shall be perfectly content living in rural isolation away from the stink and crush of London.'

Now she had astonished the company. 'How extraordinary! I never thought to meet a young lady who did not enjoy a ball or masquerade. My brother has made the perfect choice for he has little fondness for parties either.'

Her aunt lost interest in the subject and her cousin, because of her imminent departure, was naturally subdued. The conversation over luncheon was on more general subjects and then they turned to the interesting problem of the baby in the nursery.

'How long does the duke intend to keep this child under his roof? Surely after two weeks it is obvious no one is going to claim the infant,' Aunt Faith said as she wiped her mouth with a napkin.

'If the baby had been a newborn or dressed in rags it would be easier to understand how he came to be in Green Park that morning. However, he was well looked after and his nightgown and shawl were made from expensive stuff.'

'Charity, my dear, there is one explanation you have not considered, but I think it not a topic for conversation with unmarried ladies present.' Lady Annabel nodded towards her aunt who immediately pointed to the door.

'Patience, you and your cousin must go upstairs again. I wish to speak to Lady Annabel in private.'

Her cousin departed at once but Charity remained where she was. Richard was nothing to do with either of the married ladies, he was her concern and she was not going to be fobbed off like this. 'Richard was found by me and is therefore my business. Tell me at once, my lady, where you think he came from.'

'Very well, I suppose it is hardly fair

to exclude you and you will be married yourself shortly. I think it quite possible your foundling is the child of a well-to-do, unmarried girl. If her disgrace was discovered by a parent or guardian then the child would have been cast out.'

'Put in the park like a stray dog? I cannot believe a family member could treat a baby related to them in such a cruel fashion.' She closed her eyes and steadied her breathing. The thought that her darling Richard had actually been deliberately abandoned by his real family, and not abducted, was quite shocking. 'Now I come to think of it, he was placed in such a position that the first person who came past would see him. Only the wealthy take that route, so I believe the baby was put there in the hope that somebody like me would find him.'

'I doubt that anyone else would have taken him into their home as you and Hugo have, but he would have been taken somewhere safe and looked after.

However, it is likely the baby would have been found a decent home and not put in the Foundling Hospital.'

Lady Annabel was correct. Whoever had picked up the baby was likely to have provided a safe life for him. 'That means that we can keep him. As soon as we are married we will adopt him and until then we will love him as our own.'

The older women exchanged worried glances. Her aunt spoke first. 'My idea was only a suggestion. Until you have proof positive, the baby cannot be adopted. Also, my dear, are you sure the duke wishes to adopt a child born out of wedlock?'

'We haven't discussed the possibility, but I'm sure he will agree with me. We both love the baby and would be loath to part with him, unless it was to his loving parents, of course.'

She stood up. All this talk about the baby made her want to spend time with him. 'Lady Annabel, if Hugo has gone to Essex he will not be back for dinner tonight. Shall I remain in my apartment again this evening?'

'I have ordered a more elaborate dinner to be served in the grand dining room; I should like you to attend.' She smiled winningly at Aunt Faith. 'Can I count on you and your daughter?'

'She does not deserve to come down, but in the circumstances I can hardly refuse. I take it there will be no further guests?'

'Absolutely not, a delicious meal served for family only. I believe the girls have a wardrobe full of new gowns, it would be a pity if Lady Patience does not have the opportunity to wear one of them before she leaves them behind.'

Her unfortunate cousin was not only to be bundled back to Essex in disgrace but was to be forced to abandon her fashionable ensembles as well. Small wonder Patience was so despondent. She excused herself and left the married ladies to chat companionably.

She found her cousin lurking at the top of the stairs. 'If I were not so miserable, I would be elated for you, cousin. Are you to be married very soon?' Patience rattled on without waiting for an answer. 'If you are, could I prevail upon you to invite me to stay with you indefinitely? Papa can hardly refuse the request of the Duke and Duchess of Edbury.'

'I had no idea until just now that he had gone to speak to Papa. We agreed that we would be wed in June, I am to experience the horrors of the Season before I'm allowed to escape to the countryside again.'

'Will you take a wedding trip? If you don't, I could come back with you after your nuptials.'

'We have yet to discuss the details, dearest, but I doubt very much whether my husband would welcome visitors for the first few weeks of our marriage. Also, we will be moving to the north immediately and I doubt you would wish to stay there with us. There will be no parties, no gentlemen callers and no assemblies for you to attend.'

Her cousin pouted. 'In which case, I

might as well remain in Essex.' Then her sunny smile returned. 'I expect Papa will have forgiven me by then and I shall be allowed to do as I please once more. No, do not look so disapproving, I give you my word I will never entangle myself in such nonsense again.'

'I'm relieved to hear you say so. Now, I don't believe you have met Richard. I'm going to the nursery, do you care to accompany me?'

Patience shuddered theatrically. 'I do not, I've had more than enough to do with babies at home. I shall enjoy the respite whilst I can.'

They parted at the nursery stairs and Charity hurried to find the infant she hoped one day would become her son.

* * *

'Marry my daughter? How can that be? You barely know her, and I have no wish for her to move to the wilds of Northumbria where I shall never see her again.' Mr Lawson put down his spectacles and rubbed his eyes.

'I know this must be a shock to you, sir, but Charity and I are in love and wish to spend the rest of our lives together. I have been frank with you, explained that I am obliged to sell the bulk of my estates in order to clear my debts, but I will not be destitute. Your daughter will live a comfortable life and your grandchildren will not do without. I would prefer to remain in Surrey, but that is impossible.'

Mr Lawson sniffed and blew his nose loudly. 'I will not stand in the way if you have both set your hearts on this match, your grace. Mrs Lawson will not be best pleased by the news, we are both devoted to our eldest child and she is a comfort and help to both of us.'

'Thank you, sir, for your cooperation in this matter. Charity wishes you to marry us — is that possible?'

'I cannot walk my daughter down the aisle and marry her too. Perhaps you could escort her? It would be unusual, but not unheard of.'

When the interview had begun, Hugo had doubted he would get permission. Now they were discussing the details of the ceremony and everything was falling into place. 'I can't think of anything I would like more. I wish my future wife to experience a London Season before we move to Northumbria. If you would agree, we wish to be married at the beginning of June.'

'Excellent, excellent — the perfect time of year. Perhaps you would allow our daughter to return home for a week or two before you marry?'

'I give you my word that she will be with you at the beginning of May. I cannot think she will wish to stay in Town a moment longer than she has to. Unlike most young ladies she does not view a London Season with delight.'

This remark made his companion chuckle. 'She's a country girl at heart, your grace, and will do very well in Northumbria. I just wish it were not so far away.'

'I hope that you and your family will

come and make an extended stay with us once we are settled. The house is not overlarge, but quite big enough to accommodate you all with comfort.'

They chatted of inconsequential matters for a while and then he thought he would cause no offence if he departed. Hugo was determined to be back in Town before dinner — even if he had to spring his team. Since the snow had melted the weather had turned remarkably clement, the going was firm and his horses were fresh. He had driven himself in his curricle, had no retainers with him, and completing the thirty miles within the required time would present no difficulty to an experienced whipster.

He had expected Charity's father to be delighted his daughter was to marry a duke but the gentleman in question had been underwhelmed by the information. If he was honest, Mr Lawson was more worried about his beloved daughter moving so far away, than he was impressed by being the future father-in-law of The Duke of Edbury.

His horses had been well taken care of in his absence, they had been rubbed down, fed and watered and were well rested after their journey to Essex. He tossed a coin to the stableboy and sprung onto the box. He snapped his whip and the matched bays surged forward into the traces and his vehicle shot forward.

With luck he would be back before dark and just have time to change for dinner. The meal was to be a celebration of his betrothal, champagne was to be drunk and three courses and several removes were to be served. His heart pounded at the thought of seeing his beloved again in an evening gown. His mouth quirked at the thought of the dozens of new outfits provided by his aunt; at least he would not have to dip into his pocket for gowns for several years to come.

Charity had inherited the ensembles intended for her cousin. As there would be little opportunity for such finery in

Northumbria he was determined she would attend as many prestigious events as possible before they married. He wanted everyone to know this was a love match and he intended to spend every moment possible at her side.

The curricle clattered into the stable yard at dusk and two grooms were waiting to take care of his exhausted animals. If he didn't hurry he would be obliged to eat dinner in his disarray, there was barely a quarter of an hour before the gong would be sounded.

★   ★   ★

Charity stood in front of the long glass, her eyes wide in amazement. 'I cannot believe what a difference an expensive gown can make to one's appearance, Patience. I hardly recognised myself in this delightful confection.'

Her cousin was wearing a pale pink silk with a heart-shaped neckline and tiny puffed sleeves. This gown was set off by the darker pink sash and exquisite roses were scattered around the hem and neck-line. Charity's gown was cut to a similar pattern, but in blue. With matching slippers, elbow-length gloves and shawl, she could have stepped straight out of a fashion plate. Fortunately the swelling on her hand had now completely gone.

'Forget-me-not blue exactly matches your eyes, Charity, and is the perfect choice for you. The dark blue bugle beads complement the colour perfectly. I love the way your girl has dressed your hair tonight — it makes you look much older and so elegant.'

'Thank you, I think, and you look quite beautiful too. When you do eventually come and stay with us I shall give you back your gowns. I shall never wear all the ones I own, let alone your wardrobe too.'

'Shall we go down? I believe I heard Mama pass by an age ago.'

'You go, Patience, I still have to put on my slippers and find my wrap. It wouldn't do to upset your mother when she has been kind enough to allow you downstairs tonight.'

Within a few minutes she was ready and glided from the room for the first time in her life feeling like a woman grown. The tinkle of glasses and the murmur of voices drifted up from the drawing room. Why was she so nervous? Was it because she was now the future mistress of this establishment? A lot would be expected of her and she prayed she would not fail and disappoint her future husband.

She paused at the top of the stairs to catch her breath, make sure the loop of material around her wrist was securely holding her demi-train, and then she was ready to descend. She was halfway down when a figure stepped from the shadows.

She almost missed her footing. Hugo stood before her dressed in evening rig, his silver waistcoat setting off a waterfall of snowy cravat and white shirt. He looked magnificent — far too good for a country girl like her.

Then he stepped closer and she saw

his expression. He was as bedazzled as she. Before she reached the bottom step he was beside her and captured her hand.

'My darling, you look so beautiful tonight. I wish to speak to you in private before we join the others. I must tell you that your father has given us permission to marry.' He produced a small velvet box from behind him and flicked it open.

'I sent for the family betrothal ring. I want you to wear it tonight.'

He slipped the magnificent diamond over her knuckle and then raised her hand to his lips. The touch of his mouth on her hand sent a rush of unexpected heat around her.

'Please, your butler is watching us. I promise we will spend some time alone this evening. I, too, have something interesting to impart, but that can wait until after dinner.'

16

As soon as Hugo led her into the drawing room the conversation stopped and the three occupants turned to face them. Immediately the footman poured champagne into glasses and offered them round. Charity had never tasted this expensive drink; indeed, she rarely had the opportunity to drink any sort of alcohol.

Hugo put his arm around her waist and drew her close to his side; she hesitated when the tray of crystal glasses with their sparkling content was offered to her and glanced nervously upwards. He nodded and smiled encouragement, so she took a glass.

'Tonight is a special night, we are celebrating our betrothal. She has made me the happiest of men by agreeing to become my wife. We will be marrying in Essex in June.'

Everybody present already knew this information so the announcement was redundant — however, they all raised their glasses at his command. The toast done, she took no more than a sip as she discovered she wasn't overfond of the taste of champagne. Then the glasses were discarded and he led her proudly through the double doors halfway down the chamber, across the corridor and into the grand dining room.

This was the first time she'd entered this room and she was impressed by its size and elegance. The enormous table was covered with a snowy-white damask cloth, the silver was polished and the crystalware glittered in the candlelight.

Fortunately, the butler had had the sense to place them all at one end and not space them around the table so they would have been obliged to shout at each other in order to converse.

There were two chairs at the head of the table and Hugo indicated she should take the left-hand seat. His sister was to sit on his right and her aunt and cousin to take the chairs on the other side. As there were not sufficient footmen to go round they were left to seat themselves. Once they were settled the first course was brought in by three nervous parlourmaids whilst the lone footman dealt with the wine and the butler supervised placement of the dishes.

The food was not to be served to them but placed in perfect symmetry down the centre of the table and then they were to help themselves to whatever they wanted. There were eight dishes to select from and her mouth watered in anticipation.

She was determined to try a little of everything, but leave room for whatever came next. The conversation flowed easily and much was said about the forthcoming Season and the capture of the villain Napoleon Bonaparte.

By the time the second course and the dessert course had come and gone she was almost too full to move. She waited for Lady Annabel to indicate the ladies should retire but the lady smiled and indicated that for tonight this task was hers.

'Shall we retire to the drawing room, ladies, and leave the gentleman to his port?'

'You will do no such thing, sweetheart, for I have no intention of mouldering here and leaving four beautiful women on their own.'

The touch of his hand on her bare shoulder sent a thrill of anticipation around her already overheated body. As they strolled into the drawing room she found herself asking him a most impertinent question. 'I thought you were short of funds, your grace, how is it that every chamber has a fire and we were served the most expensive dinner tonight? Has there been an upturn in your fortunes?'

No sooner were the words spoken than she regretted them. His eyes narrowed and his arm tensed beneath her hand. Should she apologise immediately?

'No, my dear, I am still as destitute as I was this morning. However, as my lawyers have already found a buyer for my estates I thought we should have a proper celebration to mark our engagement.' His tone was civil but she detected his annoyance.

His words were like a bowl of cold water being thrown over her head. 'I do most sincerely beg your pardon for asking such a question. My tongue ran away with me, I believe the glass of claret I had with my dinner is to blame for my temerity.'

She expected him to smile and to be forgiven but he continued to look at her disapprovingly. 'In which case, my dear, I shall ensure that you never drink alcohol again.'

Her hand dropped from his arm and he made no attempt to retrieve it but walked on without her. She was tempted to run away, to hide her upset in the privacy of her bedchamber, but she had agreed to marry this autocratic man and must learn to deal with his set-downs if she was not to spend half the time in tears.

A hand of whist was suggested, and

as she didn't play cards, she was left to her own devices whilst the others settled comfortably around the card table. There was a piano at the far end of the room; if she played quietly nobody else would be disturbed.

She raised the lid and ran her fingers across the keys. This was a grand instrument indeed, it had been tuned recently, unlike the one she was obliged to use at home. Although she considered her singing voice was nothing out of the ordinary, she loved to play and those that listened were always generous in their praise. She had no need to find music, she could play a dozen or more sonatas by heart.

As soon as she started she was lost in her own world, forgetting her disquiet and the fact that she had fallen in love with a man she barely knew.

* * *

Hugo was playing cards like an automaton, he was famous for his skills at the table and had no need to engage his brain to come up trumps every time. The inconsequential chit-chat of the ladies drifted over his head. He wished he hadn't been so terse with Charity. He must remember she was an unsophisticated girl scarcely out of the schoolroom, whilst he was a mature man of one and thirty.

As his thoughts drifted he gradually became aware that the faint sound of the most exquisite music was haunting him. He dropped his cards face upwards, heedless of the exclamations of displeasure from his sister who was partnering him, and twisted in his seat. His beloved was at the pianoforte and playing like a virtuoso.

'Excuse me, ladies, I am done with cards for tonight.' He strode the length of the room and was about to interrupt then thought better of it. He leaned against the wall and closed his eyes, allowing the wonderful sound to fill his head.

'Hugo, are you quite well? You have been standing there without a word for an age.'

His head jerked up and she was smiling at him whilst continuing to play faultlessly. 'I had no idea you were a musical genius, my darling, I don't think I've heard anyone play better in my life.'

She nodded as if expecting his praise and continued to the crescendo of the piece. He glanced over his shoulder to find all three ladies were as entranced as he by the performance. He remained where he was until the final note died away then, ignoring his audience, he moved forward and lifted her from the piano stool.

'If I did not already love you to distraction, after that I would love you more. Whatever the expense, we shall take this piano with us to Northumbria.'

She placed a hand lightly on his chest. 'They say that music soothes the savage breast, and it certainly has proven efficacious in your case.' Her eyes sparkled with laughter and he was about to kiss her when there was a slight cough behind him.

'Charity, I have never heard anyone

play so beautifully. You must make sure that you take her to the Fitzwilliams' musicale next week, brother, she will be the star of the evening.'

Immediately his beloved stiffened. She looked up at him in horror. He nodded and she relaxed, trusting him implicitly. Keeping his arm around her waist he turned. 'I have no wish to parade my future wife in public, Annabel. Her talent as a pianist is only for her family to share.'

His throat thickened as Charity's eyes blazed her thanks. He would do anything for her; die for her if need be. He had never understood when poets drivelled on about love eternal and all that rot, but now he did. This slender girl, leaning so trustingly against him, was more important than even his title and estates.

'Darling, shall we take a stroll around the room? I believe you have something you wish to tell me.'

* * *

When she had told him the theory about Richard she waited for him to pour scorn on it. Instead he nodded. 'Why did I not think of that? It explains everything.'

'I was wondering if it might be a good idea to place an advertisement of some sort in *The Times*. If Richard's mother is from a good family then she, or someone close to her, might well see it. She must be distraught not knowing whether her precious son is dead or alive.'

'That might work, if I put the address of my lawyers then the whereabouts of the baby will remain a secret. If your premise is correct, then the person who tossed Richard aside might well demand him back in order to make his disappearance permanent.'

Her eyes filled at the thought that anyone might wish to murder their beautiful boy. 'Hugo, when we are married would it be possible to adopt him even if we don't know his true parentage?'

'I'm certain that if he remains unclaimed

until the summer there could be no objection from the courts. I had not expected to begin my married life with a ready-made family, but am content to do so if this is what you want.'

'I should like to visit the place where we found him again. If this premise is correct, then whoever left him there to be found must have come from nearby. Surely it would be possible to ascertain if a family vanished suddenly from a house in the vicinity?'

'We shall drive tomorrow afternoon. I wish to be seen with you, make sure that all the predatory gentlemen are aware you are my future bride.'

'I hardly think I'm in any danger of being stolen away from you, my love, I am a penniless vicar's daughter and will be of no interest to anyone predatory, I can assure you.'

His eyes darkened and she recognised the signs of passion. That strange heat pooled beneath her petticoats and she thought it wise to rejoin the others at the far end of the chamber.

The following morning she bade a tearful farewell to her cousin and repeated her promise to invite Patience to stay with them as soon as she could. A letter arrived from home which she devoured with interest. The first three paragraphs were to congratulate her on her coming marriage and to say how proud they were of her and how much her father had liked her future husband. Then there was news that so far only the older twins had succumbed to the chickenpox, but Mama expected the younger ones to be infected shortly. There was further information about various local dignitaries and the letter closed with what looked suspiciously like tear stains.

Her parents were putting on a brave face for her sake, but they were obviously devastated to think their oldest child was moving so far away from them. She hated the thought of not seeing her brothers and sisters grow up, not being part of their lives anymore. She also knew she would miss her cousins almost as badly as she would miss her siblings.

Even if Hugo wished to live in Timbuktu, she would go without hesitation. He was her future; although she would miss her family dreadfully, she could not survive without him at her side. She spent the remainder of the morning writing a reply full of light-hearted gossip and assurances that she would visit as often as she could.

As gentlemen did not eat at midday she dined alone with Lady Annabel. 'I notice that you and my brother are on first name terms already. Therefore I should like you to call me Annabel, and I shall call you Charity.'

'I believe that most families refer to their siblings and spouses by their titles — but Hugo insisted we break convention and I am now becoming used to it.'

'I gather that you are to go out for a drive with him at two o'clock. I have accepted an invitation for us this evening to a soirée that Lady Strachan is holding in honour of her son's majority. I cannot wait to see the faces of the tabbies when Hugo introduces you. He has been pursued for years by hopeful debutantes, there will be a general wailing and gnashing of teeth when they hear he is no longer available.'

She giggled. 'I'm surprised, if I'm honest, that he has not entered into matrimony years ago. I still cannot believe that he has finally decided to marry someone as humble as myself.'

'You must stop putting yourself down, my love. You are a diamond of the first water, I doubt there will be another young lady as beautiful as you in London this year. And, to answer your question, my brother wished to clear the bulk of his debts before he committed himself. Since he took over the title and properties he has made them profitable — but as he cannot clear the mortgages, they must go.'

'I shall always feel guilty that he lost his inheritance because he chose me. I wish, for his sake, that he had fallen in love with my cousin. I should have been broken-hearted, but happy he would have the funds he required.'

'I never want to hear you say that again, Charity. I would much rather my brother married for love than for convenience. I have done so myself, you have yet to meet my darling husband, but you will see we are ideally suited despite our differences. He is a commoner, but extremely wealthy, and I would be married to none other. Our only sadness is that up until now we have failed to produce a healthy child. But even if I remain childless, I will have no regrets about my choice of partner.'

Suitably chastised, Charity was forced to reconsider. 'In which case, Annabel, instead of worrying about the damage I am doing to your family I will celebrate the fact that I am making your brother happy.'

The sound of someone applauding behind her caused her to slop her coffee.

'Bravo, my love, I am glad you have finally understood the truth of the situation.' Hugo had wandered in unannounced and heard her impassioned speech. She jumped up and ran to him.

'I love you so much and I'm counting the days to our wedding so we can be together all the time.'

His voice was more growl than anything else. 'As am I, sweetheart. I think it quite possible I will insist that we bring forward our marriage.'

She pouted in a perfect facsimile of her cousin. 'Shall I not have my Season? Are you to deny me the pleasure of attending balls, parties and musicales?' She clutched her bosom and looked suitably dismayed. 'I shall never forgive you, your grace, for treating me so disgracefully.'

'You are a baggage and I shall enjoy teaching you how to behave.' His eyes glinted and her heart skipped a beat.

'Are you not to go driving this afternoon, brother? If you are, then Charity must change as she cannot accompany you in a morning gown.'

'I shall be down before the carriage is brought round; I require less than a quarter of an hour to get ready.' His bark of laughter followed her into the hall and she dashed up the stairs and into her chamber determined to complete her change in less than the stated time.

Her promenade gown of jonquil was ready to step into. The ensemble had matching spencer, boots and bonnet. However, she didn't stop to admire herself in her new finery, but ran through the building and arrived at the front door with two minutes to spare.

He was waiting for her, his caped driving coat making him look even bigger than he was. 'I'm impressed, my love, you must be the only woman in creation who can change so speedily. My curricle has only just arrived.' He held out his arm and she took it, feeling for the first time as if she truly belonged there at his side.

He lifted her on the box and tucked

the rug around her knees. 'I hope that bonnet is well secured, I should hate you to lose it in the park.' He grinned and strolled around to climb up beside her. 'Allow me to say how fetching you look today, my dear, you will be the perfect match for the daffodils in the flower beds.'

Her snort of laughter made him chuckle. 'I must admit that I am a trifle yellow, but I was assured this colour is all the rage this Season.'

'I thought that all young ladies must be dressed entirely in white muslin but am relieved you have ignored that fashion and have selected a colourful wardrobe.'

She was shocked to the core. 'Are you sure about not wearing colours? If that was the case, why did the seamstress not tell us? I'm sure the fashion plates we saw in *La Belle Assemblée* were of gowns in a variety of shades.'

'I believe those were for married women, not debutantes. However, I find white insipid and much prefer you in the gowns you have bought.'

They were rattling through the streets, along with hundreds of other like-minded folk, some intent on business, others heading for the park as they were to see, and be seen. Although he didn't stop and introduce her to anyone, he raised his hat and smiled at a variety of people and she knew herself to be thoroughly scrutinised and hopefully not found wanting.

They arrived at the place where Richard had been left but there was nothing of interest to see. 'Is it possible to leave the park in a carriage from this direction or do we have to return to the gate?'

'We can exit a little further up; do you wish me to drive around the area?'

They did this for a while but she saw nothing that might indicate Richard had once resided within the walls of one of the houses. Hugo drove them home a different route and she enjoyed the excursion.

'We are to go to a party of some sort

tonight, I am looking forward to it. This will be the first time we have been seen together. I have a beautiful evening gown in the palest green which I cannot wait to show you.'

He halted expertly outside the house and a waiting groom appeared from the archway to lead the team away. 'We shall dine at six o'clock and leave at eight. Radley, Annabel's husband, has arrived and will accompany us.' He half-smiled.

'That should make the evening interesting.'

17

Charity was reading her book in the library with Hugo sitting beside her studying the newspaper when the butler appeared with a letter on a silver salver. To her surprise the missive was for her.

'Who on earth could be writing to me here? It cannot be from my family as I only heard from them this morning.'

He chuckled. 'If you would open it we shall both know, my love. Kindly don't keep me in suspense.'

She broke the blob of wax that held the folded paper and opened it and read the contents aloud.

Dear Miss Lawson

Forgive me for writing to you, but I do so on behalf of a previous pupil. Word has reached me that you have taken in her child. We will be forever grateful that the lovely boy has found himself such kind sponsors.

My previous pupil was a foolish young lady who allowed her feelings to overcome her common sense and she found herself in trouble. She ran away from home and took refuge with myself and I supported her throughout her confinement and for nine months afterwards.

A month ago her father discovered her whereabouts and on seeing she had borne an illegitimate child he completely lost his head and said Thomas, for that is the infant's name, could not be allowed to survive and bring disgrace to his name. He tore the baby from her arms and sent his man of business to dispose of him.

I thought Thomas to be dead, so you cannot imagine my relief to discover he wasn't murdered but abandoned. I do not give you my name as I have no wish for you to contact me. Somehow I will get

*word to the country so the child's
mother is aware he is safe.*

*I shall never forget your kindness
and pray that you will do well by
him. If he is still known to you
when he has grown, please tell him
that his Mama loved him and would
have kept him with her if it had
been possible.*

'Good heavens, it is as we thought.
The poor girl, she believed her baby
dead at the hand of her own father.
Does that mean we can now keep him,
Hugo?'

'It does, he will be known as Richard
Thomas Avery. Unfortunately, he cannot
be given a title, but he will have a happy
life with us.'

'I had better go and change. There is
barely an hour before dinner. I'm surprised that Annabel and her husband
have not joined us for I'm sure I heard
him arrive an hour ago.'

At eight o'clock the carriage was
outside. For some inexplicable reason

Mr Radley and Annabel had failed to appear for dinner, although Hugo had appeared amused rather than irritated by their absence.

'Will they join us at the party? I wonder if . . . ' By this time they were bumping over the cobbles in the darkness along with what seemed like most of the *beau monde*.

'My darling girl, do you have any notion of what takes place between a couple once they are married?' Shock at his question left her speechless, he continued in the same vein. 'I'm referring to the marriage bed.'

She was barely able to squeak a response. 'I've no wish to discuss this, Mama will explain it all to me in good time.'

The carriage rocked as he transferred his considerable weight to her side. He continued as if she hadn't spoken. 'Shall we start with the basics? Have you ever seen animals mating?'

She was now burning from head to toe with embarrassment. 'Of course I have, what has that to do with the matter? Please, Hugo, can we change the subject?'

'The same process takes place between a man and a woman.'

She thought her dinner was about to return in a most unpleasant fashion. The very idea that people behaved like dogs and cats was too awful to contemplate. She was about to demand he turn the carriage round and take her home when he snatched her off the seat and placed her on his lap.

One strong arm encircled her waist and his other hand tilted her face towards him. Then his mouth covered hers and this was a kiss quite unlike the others he had given her. His lips were demanding, his tongue touching her teeth until her mouth opened and gave him entry.

Now she was burning from a different heat and instead of being repulsed by his invasion, she pressed closer and her hands buried themselves in the soft hair at the nape of his neck. After several delicious minutes his mouth abandoned hers and trailed pleasure down her neck until his mouth was inside her cloak and kissing the mound of her breast.

She was lost to all common sense, wanted something from him, but was not sure what. He raised his head from his exploration and whispered in her ear. 'That, my love, is what happens in a bedroom. When two people are in love they express it in a physical way. I cannot wait to make love to you. This is what my sister and her husband were doing and why they didn't come to dinner.'

Abruptly he set her aside and returned to his corner of the carriage. 'How many damned balls do you wish to attend before we can be wed?'

'None at all. In fact we could drive down to Essex tomorrow and my father could call the banns. I don't require bride clothes — I have more than I shall ever wear already.' A most wonderful thought occurred to her. 'What I would like above all things, my love, is to forego a wedding trip and return to London and enjoy the Season as your wife.'

His long legs reached out and her feet were trapped within his. 'I will happily attend one hundred soirées if it means I can spend the remainder of the night in your arms.'

The carriage jerked to a halt, cutting short their interesting but inappropriate conversation. The door was flung open, the steps let down, and she gasped to see the pavement had been covered by a red carpet and brilliant flambeaux stood in regimental rows outside the open front door.

Hugo jumped out and turned to lift her down. They joined the queue of partygoers and their carriage moved away, its place immediately taken by another vehicle. They must have been a considerable time edging their way forward to the steps but she had been unaware of it, had been too entranced by what was going on inside the carriage.

He held out his arm and she placed her hand on it. He smiled down at her and her heart almost burst from her chest with love. He pulled her closer. 'I love you, Charity Lawson, and you will be the most perfect duchess.'

'And you, your grace, have always been my perfect duke.'

THE END

ROMANCE IN THE AIR

Pat Posner

After ending a relationship she discovered was based on lies, Annie Layton has sworn off men. When her employers, Edmunds' Airways, tell her they're expanding, she eagerly agrees to help set up the sister company. Moving up north will get her away from her ex — and the Air Ministry official who's been playing havoc with her emotions. But Annie hadn't known exactly who she'd be working with ... Will she find herself pitched headlong into further heartache?

ANGELA'S RETURN HOME

Margaret Mounsdon

It has been years since schoolteacher Angela Banks last saw Russ Stretton, but she remembers him only too well. She'd had a massive crush on him as a teenager, and now he was back in her life. But he's carrying considerable emotional baggage, including a five-year-old son, Mikey — not to mention a sophisticated French ex-wife, who seems intent on winning him back at all costs . . .

THE LOVING HEART

Christina Green

Lily Ross becomes nursemaid to young Mary, whose widowed father runs Frobisher's Emporium in their seaside village in Devon. She loves her job caring for Mary, a good-natured and spirited child. Although Matt, her fisherman friend, worries her with his insistent love that she cannot return, other things fill her life: Mary and her adventures, the strange flower lady — and her growing feelings for her employer, Mr Daniel. But as his nursemaid she must keep her feelings to herself, or risk losing her position . . .

THE FATAL FLAW

Anne Hewland

When a young woman wakes with no memory of her identity, she is told by Charles Buckler that he has rescued her from a vicious attack during her journey to Ridgeworth to become the intended bride of his distant cousin, Sir Ashton Buckler. An impostor has taken her place, however, and she must resume her rightful position. Who can Elinor believe? Is Charles all he seems? What happened to Sir Ashton's first wife — and why does someone at Ridgeworth resent her presence?

AFTER ALL THESE YEARS

Natalie Kleinman

When Guy Ffoulkes walks into Honeysuckle Bunting's teashop after fourteen years, her world is turned upside-down. Guy was her brother Basil's best friend; she was Basil's scruffy younger sister. For Honey, though, there had always been more. Guy left Rills Ford at eighteen to go to university, kissing the top of Honey's head in a brotherly fashion. She was heartbroken . . . Now Guy has returned from Australia, a rich and successful architect — and when Honey discovers what his first local project will be, she is horrified . . .

A SUMMER IN TUSCANY

Wendy Kremer

Emma is an art restorer, sent to the de Luca estate by her boss. Delighted by the charms of Tuscany and involved in her work, the last thing on her mind is romance. But Leandro — the tall, dark and handsome owner of the estate — increasingly finds his way into her thoughts. Swearing not to mix business with pleasure, Emma struggles in vain to deny her growing feelings. However, Leandro's childhood friend Mariella wants him too — and she's prepared to go to any lengths to get him . . .